FREEDOM PASSAGE

*With love
Carol H Behrman*

CAROL H. BEHRMAN

AERODALE PRESS

FREEDOM PASSAGE

FREEDOM PASSAGE
Carol H. Behrman

Design
Gregg Hinlicky

Cover Illustration:
Gregg Hinlicky

Printed in the United States

First Edition
May 2011

Published by:
Aerodale Press
Post Office Box 1521
Toms River, NJ 08754
www.aerodalepress.com

© 2010 Carol H. Behrman

All rights reserved.
No part of this publication may be translated, reproduced, stored in a retrieval system, totally or partially adapted in any form or by any means, microfilm, photocopying, scanning or otherwise, without the prior written consent of Aerodale Press. If granted, the authorization is subject to the payment of royalty varying according to the use intended for publication.

ISBN 978-1-4507-7353-9

To my lovely granddaughter, Rose,
who lives in a big, old house at the Jersey Shore

Acknowledgments:

My writer friends in Sarasota: June Fiorelli,
Joan Hiatt Harlow, Elizabeth Wall, and Gail Hedrick,
who helped so much with this story.

The Brick, NJ Children's Writer's Group.

Most of all, my husband, Edward, whose insightful
suggestions, corrections, and steadfast love,
make all my work possible.

PROLOGUE—August, 1859

Titus gasped and struggled for breath. His lungs were about to burst. But he had to keep moving. He must not stop. He could hear the high-pitched yapping of the bloodhounds in the distance. He had hoped they would lose his scent. But still the beasts kept coming.

It seemed as though Titus had been running through the woods forever. Everything was conspiring against him. Even nature was threatening and hostile. He tripped over gnarly roots that wound around his ankles and tried to throw him down headlong. Sharp branches and twigs scratched at his face and bare arms, ripping and tearing his dark, sweaty skin.

Titus was trapped in a nightmare, the kind where he was trying to run, but couldn't. His legs were like cement blocks. He could feel his strength ebbing, like sap spilling from a tree. *Lord Amighty! He was so tired!* But somehow, he had to force himself to go on, to get away.

Away from the baying hounds who could rip him into bloody pieces with their sharp, merciless fangs.

Away from the plantation, the cotton fields, the overseer's whip, and the scars that would never heal.

Away from the master whose punishment would be more terrible than before, because this was Titus' third attempt at escape. This time, they might even hang him, as an example to others. A strapping, sixteen-year-old male was worth a heap of money. *Massa is greedy,* Titus thought, *but a slave who keeps running away doesn't have much value.* Fearfully, the teenage boy pictured the thick noose and the sturdy tree branch that awaited him if he were caught.

Driven forward by instinct and terror, Titus sped like a wild, desperate creature toward the unknown.

CHAPTER ONE

Peggy Gorman sprinted up the staircase to the third floor. She held her 1963 Beach Boys calendar under one arm, ready to tack it up in her new room. Her mother's voice followed. "Take off your shoes before you go in. I had the upstairs floors waxed yesterday while the house was still empty!" Peggy slid her hand along the smooth oak banister. She slipped out of her sneakers, and then pushed open the door at the top of the stairs.

"Oh!" Peggy gasped. This was a perfect room! It was large and sunny, and stretched the whole length of the house. There were fascinating nooks and crannies on all sides, especially where the eaves of the roof dipped down to make cozy v-shaped sections. None of her friends had anything like this. They lived either in city apartments or in small, new ranch houses in the suburbs. A house like this, built way back in 1855, was much more interesting. Imagine! She would be living in a home that was a hundred and eight years old!

Peggy gazed up at the carved wooden beams that criss-crossed the ceiling, and at the many windows lining both sides.

It was wonderful! Best of all was having the third floor to herself. No one could come in on her unexpectedly. She would hear them on the stairs first.

Not that Peggy Gorman got into much trouble. Unfortunately, she was a real "goody two shoes". "Why can't you be more like Peggy Gorman?" parents would ask their kids, making Peggy squirm.

But Peggy had a secret. Deep inside, Peggy didn't want to be good. She wanted to be bad. Not actually bad, but daring and unafraid instead of always trying to please everybody. She wished she were more like her favorite movie actresses, Elizabeth Taylor or Sandra Dee and especially Doris Day. They did what they wanted no matter what other people thought. If only Peggy could be so cool and sophisticated! Here in her attic room, she'd be able to practice doing that without having her parents walk in on her. Running to the door, she called down the stairs, "Mom, I love my room!"

"Good!" Her mother's voice floated up from the kitchen where she was cleaning and lining cupboards.

"When will the moving van get here?" Peggy's question echoed off the edges of the empty house.

"I can't hear you." Mom's voice sounded far off because the kitchen was two steep flights below Peggy's room.

"Never mind! I'm going to figure out where to put my furniture." Peggy stepped back inside and walked over to the windows on the far wall. This was the perfect place for her bed. From here, she could see the beach and the ocean beyond. There were a lot of people walking on the sand, splashing in the water, or stretched out on towels, soaking up the sun on this hot August afternoon. A dark-skinned woman wearing a wide-brimmed, floppy straw hat knelt at the water's edge picking up shells and putting them into a bright green tote bag. Two teenage boys tossed a ball back and forth. Peggy wondered if they went to the school she would be attending in September. The taller boy had dark wavy hair and looked cute, but it was hard to tell from this distance. Everyone looked small from up here. It had been the same in their fifth-floor apartment in New York City, but there Peggy had looked down on cars and taxis honking, and pedestrians hurrying along the street. Here, in Bay Point, New Jersey on the shores of the Atlantic Ocean, everyone seemed to be having a good time. The only problem was that they were all strangers. Strangers, not friends!

What if I never find new friends here? Peggy's excitement began to fade. She had always been shy and uncomfortable in new situations. This hadn't been a big problem for her in New York because she was part of a group of neighborhood kids. They had been friends almost forever. Even the prospect of starting junior high school in the fall wasn't too scary because her pals would be there, riding the subway together to their new school. But here, she would be all alone–an outsider. Just thinking about her dismal future made her shrink into herself in a tight knot of fear. She barely heard the footsteps on the stairs.

"How are you doing, kiddo?" Peggy's dad appeared, carrying a pink princess telephone.

"Not so good," Peggy told him. A trickling tear moistened her cheek. "I'm thinking about my friends back home."

"We'll visit you in New Jersey," each one had promised as they hugged and cried, and vowed that they would be friends forever, no matter how far apart they might live.

Peggy's dad scratched his head. "Where do you want this phone?"

"Over there." Peggy pointed to the place where she planned to put her bed.

"Right!" Jack Gorman strode over and plugged in the phone. Then he put his arms around Peggy and hugged her in the bear-like embrace that always made her feel safe. "Your friends will come to visit, Pumpkin. Everyone loves an excuse to go to the beach during the summer."

"I hope so! It's just that the New Jersey shore seems so far away to them," Peggy lamented. "People in New York go to Jones Beach or the Rockaways. You'd think New Jersey was in Siberia!"

"Peggy." Her dad gently kissed the top of her head. "You know why we have to make this move, don't you?"

"It's your great new job in Manasquan."

"Yes, it is a terrific job. I was lucky to get it. Besides, this seemed like a good time to leave the city."

Peggy nodded. She understood. A lot of scary things had been happening lately, not just in New York but in cities all over the country—strikes and marches and crowds protesting in the streets and public buildings, calling for equal rights. 1963 had not gotten off to a good start. Each day, there were new reports of sit-ins and violence, mostly in the South. Their handsome young president, John Kennedy, was upbeat and reassuring when he appeared on TV, but there was a growing fear of unrest and violence in cities throughout the country. Peggy's family lived in a fine, upscale Manhattan neighborhood. But they were convinced that life would be more pleasant in this quiet little shore town in New Jersey.

"You'll make new friends, Peg," her dad assured her.

That was easy for him to say, Peggy thought. He wasn't the one who would have to go to Bay Point Junior High School without knowing a single soul. She looked around her big, beautiful room and imagined all the long hours she would be spending here – alone!

CHAPTER TWO

Peggy's dad turned to leave. "I'm going to help your mom line the cupboards. Are you planning to stay up here?" he asked.

"I'm trying to decide where to put my furniture," Peggy told him.

"Good! The moving van will be here any minute."

After her dad left, Peggy walked slowly around the room. She flung open the doors of the two big walk-in closets. Then she saw another closet she had not noticed before. It was in the far corner of the room in a deep recess.

"Wow! Three closets!" Peggy strolled over to it. When she neared the closet, Peggy felt a sudden coldness that made her shiver.

There must be a draft here, Peggy thought, even as she wondered how there could be an icy draft in August.

Peggy reached out and touched the knob, and the world turned upside down. Reality was snuffed out like a candle in a storm. The room seemed to tip over at crazy angles like a dizzying ride through a funhouse. Ceiling and walls shifted and melted into a kaleidoscope of impossible shapes. Peggy felt as though she was being spun round and round in a crazy somersault. She would have screamed if she could, but she had no voice. And then, as quickly as it had begun, it all ended. Peggy found herself standing in the same place as before, while the room had returned to its original shape.

Peggy shivered. What had happened? She squeezed her eyes shut, then opened them again. Everything looked exactly as it should. The midday sun was streaming in. It lit up the room in a rosy glow of normalcy. Could she have imagined the whole thing?

That had to be the explanation. It was the excitement of the move making her see things that weren't there. *I'm not going to tell Mom,* she decided, *or she'll worry that I'm coming down with some terrible illness.* Peggy passed her palm across her forehead, wondering if maybe she was getting sick, but her temperature felt normal. Everyone gets dizzy sometimes, she thought.

Then Peggy noticed that her other hand was no longer on the knob of the closet door.

What will happen, she wondered, *if I touch it again?*

Before she could try, she heard loud noises downstairs. She ran to look out the nearest window. The moving van had arrived! Two husky guys were pulling out the Gormans' possessions. They first brought in the furniture for the third floor. Thoughts about the closet flickered away at the sight of Peggy's dear and familiar possessions. When everything was in place, she opened her suitcases and began to put clothes neatly into her dresser drawers. She placed the new record player she had gotten for her birthday on a table next to her desk, plugged it in, and stacked her records on the shelf below. Then she selected her current favorite and set it on the turntable.

What a jerk she had been to get upset over a little dizziness.

"The answer, my friend, is blowin' in the wind," she sang along with Bob Dylan, as she hung up her dresses and dungarees. Just singing along with Dylan helped Peggy feel less lonely and afraid. Her new room was great. There was more than enough space in the two huge closets for the hip stitch pleated skirts that everyone was wearing.

But even Bob Dylan couldn't keep Peggy's thoughts from returning to the corner closet. *Do I dare?* she wondered. Taking a deep breath, she walked slowly to the corner recess. It was still colder than the rest of the room. Peggy hesitated, then stretched out her hand and took hold of the knob. Nothing happened. Of course not! She had imagined the whole thing! Peggy turned the knob. The door would not open. She tugged at it, harder and harder, but it didn't budge.

It must be stuck, she thought. She went out of the room and called down to her father. "I need help, Dad."

He came up in a jiffy, trailed by Patches, their brown and orange calico cat. Peggy showed Dad the closet. He couldn't get it open either. He examined the knob and the keyhole. "It must be locked," he said. "Do you really need this closet?"

Peggy nodded.

"We'll get it open as soon as I find a key that works. Can you wait, Peg?"

"Sure." Peggy hoped she wouldn't have to wait too long. Suddenly, getting that closet door open seemed tremendously important.

Just before he left, Dad remarked, "Attics are usually hot, but not this one. In fact, it seems cooler than the rest of the house."

As Peggy watched her father saunter down the steps, she noticed that Patches hadn't come into the room. The cat was sitting just outside on his haunches, sniffing the air suspiciously.

"Come on in, Patches," coaxed Peggy. "There's nothing to be afraid of here."

Patches' ears twitched. He turned and bolted down the stairs after Peggy's dad.

CHAPTER THREE

They hadn't found the key by the time Dad went off early Monday morning to his new job. "I'll look for it tonight, Peg. I promise," he assured her.

Right after breakfast, Mom began roaming the house, darting from room to room, taking measurements, and jotting down figures in a notebook. Patches followed close on her heels, as though not wanting to lose sight of his chief meal provider in this strange new environment.

"You and I are going to spend the next few weeks decorating our house, Peggy," Mom enthused. "We're going to have great fun!"

"Great fun for *you*," Peggy whispered, too

low for Mom to hear. Peggy shuddered as she imagined herself being dragged around to furniture shops, upholsterers, and paint stores, and forced to listen to excruciating details about couches, curtains, and throw pillows.

"I'm going to go crazy. I know it!" Peggy muttered later when she was alone in her room. Her throat tightened up when she remembered her old pals, now probably gone forever. What if she never made any new friends here? She stared out the window and tried to hold back her tears. Her mother was in the front yard examining the tall, flowering bushes that separated their house from the one next door. Her mom's lips were moving and Peggy realized that she was talking to someone on the other side. Then she saw a woman slip through a gap in the bushes and accompany Peggy's mom back to the house.

Is it our next door neighbor? Peggy didn't have to wonder for long.

"Peggy, will you please come down here," her mother called, using her "company" voice.

Peggy switched off the record player. "Sorry, Bob," she apologized to Dylan. She sped down the stairs to find her mom and their visitor seated in the conservatory.

Conservatory! That's what the glassed-in room at the back of the house was called. If Peggy's friends were around, they would have had a good laugh over that name. It was a pretty room, overlooking a backyard filled with green bushes and brightly colored flowers. Mom was planning to buy wrought iron furniture and put pots of plants all around. Now, it held only a couch and a couple of chairs that would later be placed elsewhere in the house.

"Come in, Peggy," said her mother, "and meet our neighbor, Mrs. Purvis."

Mrs. Purvis was tall and slim. Her skin was cocoa-colored and smooth as satin. She wore a sleeveless, flowered shift and a big straw hat.

"I saw you on the beach yesterday," Peggy told Mrs. Purvis. "You were looking for shells."

Mrs. Purvis grinned. "Now you know my great passion," she said. "I'm a shell collector."

"There's something else," interjected Peggy's mother. "Mrs. Purvis. . ."

"Cora!" the woman corrected her.

"Well, yes, and please call me Eve." Mom turned to Peggy again. "Peggy, would you believe that Mrs. Purvis—I mean Cora—has a daughter just your age."

"Will she be going into seventh grade?" Peggy leaned forward eagerly.

Mrs. Purvis nodded. "Yes, but she's quite nervous about going to a new school. You see, we've only been here for a month."

"Where are you from?" Peggy inquired.

"Here's another coincidence, Peggy Ann," her mother exclaimed. "The Purvises used to live in New York City."

"Queens," said Mrs. Purvis. "Bay Point seems like heaven to us."

"To us, too," Mom affirmed.

"What's your daughter's name?" Peggy asked.

"Julia."

"What's Julia doing now?"

"She's at ballet school. Are you interested in dance?" Mrs. Purvis asked.

Peggy shook her head.

"Peggy is studying violin," her mother explained. "But we have to find a new teacher for her in this area."

Mrs. Purvis offered to ask her daughter's ballet teacher for a recommendation. "She knows everyone who's involved in the arts."

"That would be excellent."

Mrs. Purvis got up. "I have to go now," she said, and faced Peggy. "Would you like to come by later to meet Julia? Say, around three?"

"Can I, Mom?" Peggy begged. Her mother agreed, and Mrs. Purvis left. Peggy and her mother then began looking through swatches of material trying to choose a fabric for recovering one of their couches.

"The time won't go any faster if you keep checking your watch every five minutes," Peggy's mom remarked. She held a nubby blue fabric up to the light. "You know, I was surprised to see that a colored family is living next door."

"*Black,* Mom," Peggy corrected. "They want to be called black, not colored. It's okay that the Purvises are living next door, isn't it?"

Mrs. Gorman put down the blue swatch and picked up a green one. "Of course," she stated. "It's good to see that this town is integrated."

"Like our old neighborhood."

Peggy's mom smiled. "That's right."

"Elise Gantry is black," Peggy mused, thinking about her friends. "I miss Elise a lot already."

Peggy's mom frowned. "You know, Peggy, not every place is like upper West Side Manhattan."

"I *know* that!" Peggy hated it when her mom spoke to her as though she were a small child. "We learn stuff in school, and I see news on TV. But New Jersey isn't the South where black people are discriminated against!"

Her mother sighed. "I'm sure you're right, Peggy. After all, the Purvises seem happy in Bay Point. She picked up a silky yellow swatch. "How do you like this one?"

Peggy barely glanced at the material. "It's fine." She looked at her watch for the hundredth time. "Three o'clock!" she shouted. "I'm on my way!" Peggy bolted out the door as though shot from a cannon. She rushed next door, rang the bell, and soon was face to face with a potential new friend.

Julia Purvis looked a lot like her mother. She had thick black hair that hung in two long braids down her back, and wore a cute pink skirt and embroidered white blouse.

"You're Peggy!" Julia exclaimed. "You don't know how happy I am that you've moved in next door. Let's go to my room!"

Julia's room was on the second floor. It wasn't even half the size of Peggy's bedroom, but nicely decorated with yellow flowered wallpaper, matching curtains at the windows, and a double bed with a yellow, padded headboard. Julia went immediately to the record player on the dresser. "I've got the new Beach Boys album," she told Peggy. "It's called *Surfin' USA!*"

Julia put on the album, and for the next two hours, they sat on the bed, listening to music and discovering that they had everything in common. They adored the Drifters, Bob Dylan, Martha Reeves and the Vandellas, and even Elvis Presley, although they agreed that Elvis was not as good as he used to be.

"I did love that last movie he was in, *Girls, Girls, Girls*, said Julia, rummaging through her albums. "Here it is! Here's the soundtrack."

She put it on, and while Elvis crooned *Return to Sender*, they discovered they shared other interests, such as classical music–Peggy for the violin and Julia for ballet. They were intense Yankee fans and idolized the same players Mickey Mantle, Roger Maris and Elston

Howard. They had similar tastes in books, too. Both loved *A Wrinkle In Time* and all the Nancy Drew stories.

And Julia was wild about some of the movie stars that Peggy loved, like Elizabeth Taylor and Sandra Dee, and that adorable Bobby Darin, although her favorite was a gorgeous black actor named Sidney Poitier.

"I love your house," Julia remarked. "It's so unusual. My mom says it's real old."

"Over a hundred years," Peggy told her. "My room takes up the whole third floor."

"Wow! It must be huge!"

"It is! It's great." Peggy hesitated for a minute, and then blurted out, "But there's something strange about it!"

"Really? What?"

Peggy hadn't told anyone about her weird experience the day before. She didn't plan to ever talk about it. But suddenly she found herself relating the whole episode exactly as it had happened. When she finished, Julia didn't say a word. She just sat there, staring at Peggy.

Now I've blown it, Peggy thought. *She probably thinks I'm some kind of psycho!*

When Julia finally spoke, it was not to ridicule what had happened, as Peggy expected. Julia's eyes were dark and serious. "What's in that closet?" she asked.

Peggy nervously combed her silky, wheat-colored hair with her fingers while she pondered what Julia had said. It had never occurred to her that something might be in the closet. "I don't know. It's locked," Peggy explained, "and we couldn't find the key."

They were interrupted by the sound of a scratchy needle on the phonograph. Julia got up to turn the record over. As Elvis began another song, Peggy's new friend turned to face her.

"Oh, Peggy!" Julia exclaimed. "I'm so glad you're here. It was pathetically boring until you came!" She nodded emphatically. "And I'm going to help you find the key to that closet."

CHAPTER FOUR

The following day turned out to be one of the hottest of the summer. At ten o'clock in the morning, the temperature was already ninety degrees.

Julia telephoned and suggested they go to the beach. "It'll get too hot later," she predicted.

"Can you be ready in an hour?"

"You bet!" In ten minutes, Peggy had changed into her bathing suit and begged out of going drapery shopping with her mom. Fortunately, Peggy's mother was so delighted that Peggy had found a friend, that she gave in quickly, especially when Peggy assured her that Julia's mom would be home all day.

A lot of people were already on the beach. It was dotted with striped umbrellas, beach chairs, and towels, all in bright summer colors. Toddlers, at the edge of the water, screamed with delight as incoming waves puddled around their feet. The girls slipped off their sandals and dug their toes into the soft, squishy sand.

"Let's stay back here where it's not so crowded." Julia had brought along a large blue blanket, which she spread on the sand. A strong, ocean breeze whipped up the ends of the blanket, so the girls set their shoes and beach bags on the corners to hold it in place.

Julia patted the blanket. "Let's relax."

Peggy shook her head. "I'm going for a swim first." She gazed out at the water. It reflected the clear blue of the sky. Closer to shore, the waves crashed and broke into cascades of white foam. "You coming?"

Julia shook her head. "I wanna soak up the sun for a while." She stretched out on her back and adjusted her sunglasses. "This is so great!"

"I'll be back in a few minutes." Peggy ran toward the ocean. The hot sand stung at the soles of her feet like swarms of angry bees until she reached the shoreline, where it was wet and cool. She stepped into the cold water. "This feels good," Peggy remarked to no one in particular.

"Yeah, today is going to be a scorcher." A tall blonde girl was standing beside Peggy holding a red and white beach ball. "I haven't seen you here before."

"We just moved in," Peggy told her.

"Are you summer people?" The girl's voice held a note of condescension.

Uh oh! Peggy thought. *I guess the locals look down at people who come here just for the summer.* She was happy to be able to say, "No, we're going to live here all year."

The girl smiled, although the smile did not seem to extend to her blue eyes, which were cool and controlled. "I'm Sandra Bendix. Welcome to Bay Point."

"Thanks. I'm Peggy Gorman. Do they call you Sandy?"

"No way!" Sandra snorted. "My mother would never permit that. She hates low-class nicknames."

Peggy thought it best not to mention that Peggy was a nickname for Margaret.

"You want to toss the ball around?" Sandra threw the beach ball to Peggy, who sent it back. She couldn't believe her good luck. Here only a couple of days, and already she had met two kids! Sandra was tall, but Peggy suspected they were about the same age.

"So, where do you live?" Sandra asked.

"On Blount Street."

Sandra stopped throwing the ball and stared at Peggy. "You didn't buy that big, old Deerfield place, did you?"

"It is a big, old house. But I don't think the people we bought it from were named Deerfield."

Sandra shook her head. "Deerfields haven't lived there in a zillion years. But everybody here still calls it the Deerfield place." She began to toss the ball again. "It must be huge inside."

Peggy nodded. "It is. My room takes up the whole third floor."

"Really?" Peggy thought she detected a note of envy.

Sandra stepped closer to Peggy. "Have you seen any ghosts?" she whispered.

"What?" Now it was Peggy's turn to stop and stare.

Sandra shrugged. "Well, people do say that the Deerfield place is haunted. Have you noticed anything strange?"

"No!" Peggy replied quickly.

To Peggy's relief, Sandra immediately changed the subject. "Let's swim!" she announced. She set down the ball and ran into the water. Peggy plunged in after her. The ocean was cool and refreshing. They swam and paddled around for a while. Sandra was an excellent swimmer, much better than Peggy. *I guess that's what happens when you live at the shore*, Peggy thought.

When they emerged, dripping and laughing, Sandra said, "I've always wanted to see the inside of the Deerfield house."

"Why don't you come home with me now?" Peggy suggested.

"I'd like that."

"I just have to get my friend," Peggy told her. She headed across the beach, dodging sunbathers and children at play. Her feet were still wet so the sand didn't burn so much. Sandra followed behind.

"This will be so cool," Sandra crowed. "I'll be the first in our crowd to get inside the Deerfield house."

"It's the Gorman house now," Peggy declared, as she reached Julia's blanket. "Julia, meet Sandra."

Julia sat up. She removed her sunglasses and blinked at the two girls standing over her. "Hi." There was no reply. Peggy turned to look at Sandra. She was staring at Julia with narrowed eyes and pinched lips.

"I won't be able to go with you after all," she told Peggy in a cold, clipped voice. "I think my friends are looking for me." She turned her back and began to walk in the direction of a group of girls who were standing a short distance away, watching them.

"Wait a minute!" Peggy ran after her. "When do you want to come see my house?"

Sandra looked at Peggy, her face as hard as granite. "If I were you," she hissed, "I'd be careful who I hang out with, if you want to be liked in Bay Point." She strode off, leaving Peggy astonished and confused. She ran back to Julia, who was still sitting on the blanket. "What just happened?" she wondered aloud.

Julia put her sunglasses back on. "Don't you

know?"

"No." Peggy was bewildered. Everything had been so great just a few moments ago. She didn't understand why it had changed.

"That girl hates me," Julia's voice trembled with emotion.

"But Julia," Peggy insisted, "why would Sandra hate you? She doesn't even know you."

"She sees my color," Julia said bitterly. "That's all she needs to know."

So that was it! Julia believed that Sandra was prejudiced. In New York, Peggy's friends had been of all colors and ethnic origins. Their big joke was that West Side Manhattan was a regular United Nations. Of course, Peggy had watched news programs that showed black people being discriminated against. But those things didn't happen here, did they? Right now, Peggy just wanted to make Julia feel better. "We don't really know what Sandra meant," Peggy suggested. "Maybe she just saw her friends and wanted to talk to them."

Julia shook her head. She rose heavily, as though she had suddenly become old and weary. "I know it." She began to fold up the blanket. "Maybe it would be better for you not to be seen with me."

For a moment, Peggy hesitated, wondering if Julia was right. Then she brushed off that feeling and grabbed one side of the blanket to help Julia finish the job. "You're my friend, Julia. I feel as though I've known you forever. Don't you feel that way, too?"

Julia nodded. "I just don't want to get you in trouble with the kids here."

"Sandra's only one person," Peggy pointed out. "That doesn't mean the other kids are the same."

"Well, maybe." Julia didn't sound convinced.

"Let's get out of here," Peggy suggested. "I think it's time we investigated that closet of mine."

Julia brightened immediately. "Right on!" she said. "Let's go for it!"

They headed back towards home and changed out of their bathing suits. Peggy could see that Julia was still disturbed about their encounter on the beach but didn't want to talk about it. Instead, they concentrated on their new quest.

First, Julia tried to open the closet door, and

was as unsuccessful as Peggy and her father had been.

"It's locked!" Peggy reminded her.

"Your dad hasn't found the key yet?" Julia asked.

Peggy shook her head. "I don't think he's looked that hard. He's had a million other things to do."

Julia bit her lip thoughtfully. "Maybe it's hidden somewhere in this room."

"Why would anyone hide a key to a closet?"

"Well, we don't know what's inside, do we?" Julia pointed out.

The girls began to comb the room carefully, looking for the key. They examined every wall, peered into each nook and crevice, but came up empty-handed.

Julia sighed with disappointment. "I was so sure it would be here."

"We haven't looked in the other closets," Peggy pointed out. "I'll take one and you take the other."

Peggy moved all the hangers together so that her garments were stacked in the middle of the clothes rod. She began to search the side walls, moving her hands along them from top to bottom so as not to miss a single spot. Then she did the same on the rear wall. In the lower right corner near the floor, she felt a bump. "Come here," she called, excitedly.

Julia dashed over. "What?"

"Feel this bump?"

Julia squatted on the floor next to Peggy and put her hand on the spot. "Yes."

"I think there's something underneath. We'll have to break through." Peggy looked around. "What can we use?"

"Do you have anything sharp?" asked Julia.

Peggy reached into her pocket and pulled out her own house key. "Maybe this will work." She began to pound and scratch with the point of the key, trying to crack through the plaster. "My dad is going to kill me if he sees this," she commented, as little by little the plaster flaked off. Finally, the entire bump fell off, landing in little white pieces on the bottom of the closet.

There, nestled in the corner where the wall met the floor, lay a small, black key.

"We found it!"

Peggy picked up the key and brushed away

the bits of plaster that still clung to it. It lay in the palm of her hand, cool and mysterious. "We don't know for sure that it will open that closet," she pointed out.

"Of course it will!" Julia exclaimed. "Why else would there be a locked closet and a hidden key in the same room?" She jumped up. "Let's try it!"

Peggy didn't answer. Feeling the cold metal of the key upon her hand had brought a sudden premonition of danger, a sense of something strange and unnatural.

"What are you waiting for?" Julia exclaimed impatiently.

The sound of Julia's voice, happy and excited, helped Peggy shrug off her weird sensation. She got up, strode over to the mysterious closet, and inserted the key. It fit perfectly. Slowly, Peggy turned the key in the lock. With a click, the door swung open, and the girls found themselves staring into the dimness of a small, windowless chamber.

"It's not a closet at all!" Julia exclaimed. "It's a little room."

They stepped into the small, rectangular

room. It was empty, and there was a stale, musty odor, as though fresh air had not entered in a long, long time.

"I wonder what this was used for?" murmured Julia.

Before Peggy could reply, there was a click behind them as the door suddenly swung shut and they were plunged into darkness. And then it happened again–the terrifying sense of falling and spinning out of control in a whirling tunnel of shifting colors. She could hear Julia screaming as though from a great distance. *We're going to die!* Peggy thought, but once again, the terror ended as quickly as it had begun. Peggy found herself standing next to Julia in the hidden room.

But it was not the same as before! The room was different. It smelled different, it felt different, and it looked different. There was freshness in the air like a scrubbed-clean space, and the sense of a home where people lived. The area was now lit by a lantern that stood on a small round table in the center of the room. On the far wall was a narrow cot.

And someone else was in the room! A short, stout

woman stood next to the cot holding a pillow and folded sheets in her arms. Her grey-streaked hair was pulled into a neat bun at the back of her neck. She wore an old-fashioned white blouse and a long gray skirt that trailed on the floor.

As Peggy's heart pounded with fear, the woman's weary, blue eyes gazed straight at her. "Stop dawdling girls," she said, "and come help me make up this bed."

Peggy turned to look at Julia, and gasped. Julia was no longer wearing her regular clothes. She was dressed like the strange woman, except that her long skirt was brown.

So was Peggy's. She, too, was clad in garments from long ago.

"Hurry, girls!" said the woman. "You must do your part in our blessed enterprise. He will be arriving at any moment."

CHAPTER FIVE

Am I dreaming? Peggy wondered. She grasped Julia's hand. It was warm and real. The girls looked in each other's eyes and each saw her own fear and bewilderment reflected there. *This was no dream! This was really happening!* Holding hands tightly, they advanced cautiously toward the cot where the woman was waiting for them.

"Don't look so frightened," the woman said. "He won't hurt you, poor, unfortunate fellow that he is." She set the pillow upon the bed and placed the sheets in Julia's hands. "Here, you girls can manage this yourselves. I'm going to bring up some food. He'll be mighty hungry."

She walked gracefully across the room, her long skirt trailing on the floor, opened the door, disappeared, and closed the door behind her. Julia caught a glimpse of the room beyond in the few seconds the door was open. It was her bedroom, but nothing of hers was still there. Instead, it seemed to be a storage area crammed with boxes and trunks.

Stiff and terrified, moving like robots, the girls began to make up the bed. At first, they were too stunned to talk, or even to think. Julia finally broke the silence. "Where are we?" she whispered. "Are we dead?" She looked around the room. "This isn't my idea of heaven, girl." Peggy tucked in the corners of the bed sheet. "I. . .I'm not sure," she stammered in confusion. "I don't think we're dead because we're still in the same house."

"Doesn't look the same," Julia sighed. They stared at their surroundings and at each other.

"Did you see the way that woman was dressed?" Peggy's voice squeaked with fear and excitement.

Julia pointed to their own clothes. "And look

at us!" she exclaimed.

The long skirts felt strange around their ankles. Their snowy-white blouses were stiffly starched and buttoned tightly at the neck and wrists.

Could it be? Had they gone back in time? Peggy wondered. They were silent for a few moments. Then Julia uttered the words they were both thinking. "I don't think it's 1963 any longer. We've got to get out of here!"

Before Peggy could reply, they heard a murmur of voices and the sound of heavy footsteps upon the stairs.

"This way." Peggy recognized the voice of the woman in the grey skirt.

The door opened and three people entered. The woman came first, bearing a tray of food, which she placed upon the table. She was followed by a tall man who wore a roughly woven black suit and a knit fisherman's cap. Behind him came a muscular teenager with glistening black skin and terrified dark eyes. His pants were torn and filthy. He wore a black shirt that was too tight to have been his. It stretched across his big chest.

"This here is Titus." The man's voice was gruff, but not unkind.

"Tell Titus that he is kindly welcome to our station, girls," instructed the woman.

"Welcome Titus," they said in unison, as Peggy wondered, *station?* The only stations she knew were stops on the New York subway system.

The boy bowed his head. "Thankee," he replied in a trembling voice, keeping his gaze fixed on the floor.

"You must be tired and hungry, Titus," said the woman.

He nodded, still looking down. "Yes'm, ah'm mahty starved, and thassa fact."

"Didn't you give him anything to eat?" The woman stared accusingly at the fisherman.

He shook his head. "The boy came charging out of the woods like a stuck deer. He said the bloodhounds were on his trail. It was all we could do to put him in the boat and get out of there as fast as we could."

"So, you haven't eaten either?"

He nodded.

"And your crew the same?"

"Yes ma'am."

She sighed. "Well, God bless all of you, Josiah. You are good people. Come down to the kitchen and I'll put out a spread for you."

Titus began to follow Josiah out the door.

"Not you, Titus!" she cautioned. "It would be too dangerous for you to be seen. There's talk around town about slave hunters who are eager to pick up runaways and collect their ill-gotten reward."

Titus backed up and seemed to tremble even more.

"I've brought you some nourishment." She pointed to the tray of food on the table. "Eat and drink, Titus, but don't leave this room. I'll be up again shortly to tell you what the next leg of your journey will be. Meanwhile, eat and then rest."

"Yes'm." He sat down at the table and immediately began to stuff food into his mouth.

The woman turned to the fisherman. "Let's go down to the kitchen where you can sup and rest." She opened the door.

"Thankee Missus Whitehead." The fisherman went out of the room.

Mrs. Whitehead walked after him, calling behind her, "Come now, girls, let us feed these brave, godly men. And be sure to push the big steamer trunk against the door."

Still staring at Titus, who was wolfing down his meal as though he hadn't eaten in days, Peggy and Julia backed out of the room. The door closed.

They turned around and gasped in amazement. Mrs. Whitehead was gone. So was the fisherman.

Peggy's bedroom was exactly as they had left it just a few minutes before. I… ."I.....think we're home," she stammered.

Julia looked back at the closet. She put her hand on the doorknob.

"No!" Peggy screamed. "Don't open that door."

Julia pulled back her hand as though she had been bitten by a rattlesnake. "You're right." She reached for the key that was still in the lock, and turned it until it clicked into place. "What just happened to us, Peggy?"

Peggy shook her head. "Darned if I know." She examined her clothes. They were what she had been wearing earlier—normal, 1963 clothes. "If I didn't know it was impossible, I'd say that we went back in time."

Julia's eyes flashed with excitement. "It's like that movie, *The Time Machine*, with Rod Taylor. Did you see it?"

Peggy nodded. "Yes, I saw *The Time Machine*." She remembered how exciting it had been. But it was make-believe! An image of Titus swept into Peggy's mind. Titus, his dark skin sweating, his eyes sharp with terror. Titus had been real. "That was just a movie," Peggy pointed out. "There's no such thing as a machine that can travel through time."

"Even if there was, we sure don't have one," Julia said.

Peggy thought about the awful, spinning, falling sensation when they opened the closet door. "Maybe that whole room is a time machine."

A door opened and shut downstairs. The voice of Peggy's mom came floating up the stairs. "Peggy, are you up there?"

The girls were still standing near the locked closet. Quickly, they moved away. Peggy stared at Julia. "What do I tell my Mom?" she whispered.

"Nothing!" Julia shook her head vehemently.

"You don't think anyone is going to believe us, do you?"

"You're right," Peggy agreed. "They'll say we made the whole thing up."

"Or had a hallucination."

Peggy shuddered. "They'll send us to a shrink."

"Peggy!" Her mother's voice was louder and more insistent.

Peggy managed to call out a reply, although her throat felt as tight as if it had been stitched shut. "We're in my room, Mom! Julia's here."

"I'll be in the kitchen. Is Julia staying for lunch?"

Peggy looked at her friend inquiringly. "I'm not going anywhere," Julia told her.

"She's staying," Peggy called.

"Okay, come down in about half an hour." Her mom's voice trailed off as she headed for the back of the house.

"We've got to get this straight ourselves first before we talk to anyone else," Julia advised. "What do you think happened, Peggy?"

"We went back in time." It had to be true! What other explanation was there? "But where were we, and what was happening? Who were those people?"

"I've been thinking and thinking about this ever since that door closed behind us." Julia sank down onto the soft, fluffy area rug near Peggy's bed and pulled Peggy down beside her. "I remembered a book my mom gave me to read last year. Did you ever hear of the Underground Railroad?"

Peggy nodded. "It sounds familiar. Wasn't that something they had before the Civil War?"

"Yes," said Julia. "That's what this book was about. Back when there were slaves in this country, some were desperate enough to run away. There were people who helped them escape up north or to Canada where they could be free. They hid them in houses along the way."

"She said *station*," Peggy mused, "that Mrs. Whitehead."

"That's what they called the stops along the Underground Railroad."

Peggy shook her head. Her brains felt scrambled trying to figure out what had happened. "But that was so long ago."

"More than a hundred years," Julia agreed.

Peggy jumped up and went over to her

record player. "Music helps me think," she explained.

"Me too," Julia agreed. "But all the thinking in the world isn't going to tell us for sure what's happening here. There's only one way to find out."

"How?"

"We've got to go back into that room again."

CHAPTER SIX

"You've got to be kidding!" Peggy stared at Julia as though her friend had lost her mind. "What if the same thing happens again?"

"What if it doesn't?" Julia countered.

Peggy thought that over while the Beach Boys belted out *Surfin' USA* in the background. "If nothing weird happens, then we'll know we imagined it."

In her heart, Peggy knew she had not imagined that strange journey, and she was convinced Julia felt the same.

"Lunch is ready, girls!" Her mother's voice came as a relief, reminding Peggy that some things were still the same, still normal.

Peggy touched her lips with her forefinger. "Remember!" she warned Julia as they began walking down the steps, "not a word!"

"Not a word!" Julia agreed.

It was hard not to talk about the thing that crowded Peggy's mind like an unruly mob. Several times during lunch, Mrs. Gorman asked why the girls were so quiet.

"I guess we're tired from the beach," Peggy told her.

Julia had to leave right after lunch to get ready for a ballet lesson.

"Tomorrow!" Julia whispered as she was going out the door.

"Tomorrow," Peggy agreed.

She was in her room later looking out the window and trying to keep her gaze away from the closet when she noticed three kids walking on the sidewalk. They turned into her driveway and came to the front door.

One of them was Sandra. She did not know the other two.

When the bell rang, Peggy sprinted down the stairs with the speed of a gold-medal racer. "I'll get it," she shouted to her mother, who was working in a small bedroom on the second floor she now called the "sewing room".

Peggy flung open the front door. "Come in."

Sandra stepped forward followed by a short, chunky girl and a tall, dark-haired boy who seemed somehow familiar.

"You said that I could see your house," Sandra said. She had a way of speaking that was almost royal, as though no one would dare disagree with her.

Peggy was so happy that she didn't mind Sandra's lofty tones. "Sure!" She tried to imagine herself into a self-assured Doris Day mode, but heard her own voice coming out cracked and timid.

"This is Kimberly." Sandra indicated the stocky girl. Kimberly had a halo of golden curls, and when she smiled, she looked like a chubby angel.

"I'm Pete," added the boy. Peggy realized why he seemed familiar. She had seen him playing ball on the beach the other day.

"Well, are you going to give us the tour?" Sandra asked.

Peggy began to show them around the house, but Sandra stopped at the foot of the stairs. "I want to see that third floor," she insisted.

The third floor? Fear clutched at Peggy's heart like an iron fist. Did Sandra know about the closet?

"I hear that your room is huge," Kimberly remarked.

The iron fist relaxed its hold on Peggy's chest and she breathed a sigh of relief. It was just the room! They wanted to see Peggy's room!

"C'mon." Peggy led them up the stairs. When they reached the second floor, Peggy's mom came out to greet the visitors.

"We're going to look at my room," Peggy told her, as they climbed the flight of stairs that led to Peggy's part of the house.

Sandra went in first. She looked around without comment. But Kimberly exclaimed, "Wow! This is all yours?"

Peggy nodded.

"It's so private!" Peter sounded impressed.

Sandra still hadn't said anything. She walked around the room, peering at Peggy's things. When she reached the closet in the far corner, Peggy's heart missed a beat. Luckily, Sandra passed the closet without comment and continued around the room until she was back near the entrance. "This room is too big," she finally announced. "I like something cozier."

"You're just jealous," said Kimberly, who then seemed to shrink into herself when Sandra darted a knife-like, piercing look at her.

Peggy tried to think of something clever to say, but her lips seemed to be glued together.

"Let's go," Sandra announced, and she strode down the stairs. The others followed meekly, with Peggy bringing up the rear.

At the front door, Sandra turned to Peggy. "By the way," she said, "do you want to hang out with us at the beach tomorrow morning?"

Peggy's spirits rose immediately, like bubbles floating into the stratosphere. "Sure," she replied. "That would be great."

"We'll see you there at ten." Sandra went out. Kimberly and Pete followed, but Pete stopped first and managed to say, "See you tomorrow," before Sandra pulled him away.

Peggy watched them walk off. She was so elated that she was almost able to put the closet incident out of her thoughts, until dinner that evening when her dad brought it up.

"I haven't been able to locate the key," he said, spearing a cube of lamb. "I might have to bring in a locksmith to get it open."

Peggy almost choked on the baby carrot she was chewing. "No!" she exclaimed quickly. "I found the key."

Her father looked at her with interest. "Where?"

"In one of the other closets."

"Well, I'll be!" He grinned. "That was very resourceful of you, Pumpkin."

Peggy nodded, getting more nervous by the moment. What if they asked her what was in the closet? She wasn't good at lying. Her parents always knew when she wasn't telling the truth.

Fortunately, her dad changed the subject. "Well," he commented, "that's one less thing to worry about. Did I tell you about the problem we have with the garage door?"

Peggy breathed a sigh of relief. Her secret was safe for the moment. But she was restless when she went to bed that night. Her mind was a whirl of activity. One moment, she was filled with excitement thinking about the invitation she had received earlier. Then she glanced in the direction of the closet and shuddered as she relived that scary, dizzying fall into another time. When she heard a scratching sound nearby, she sat up, frozen with terror. *Maybe something had escaped from that closet—something horrible from a distant time and place!*

Trembling, afraid to move, Peggy somehow managed to reach over and turn on her bedside lamp. She looked all around in a panic, but saw nothing. Then the scratching started again. This time, Peggy realized that it came from outside the door to her room. A faint mewing provided an answer to the mystery. Peggy scrambled out of bed and opened the door. Patches stood there, his green eyes brilliant in the dim light.

"Come in, Patches." In their old house, the cat had always slept at the foot of Peggy's bed, but here, he had refused to even enter Peggy's room. The animal looked at Peggy accusingly. It was clear he wanted the comfort of sleeping in the usual spot. But still he stayed at the edge of the threshhold, unwilling to cross it.

"It's okay, Patches." Peggy leaned down to pet the cat. He stretched his body luxuriously under her hand and began to purr, but when Peggy tried to pull him inside, he resisted, bristling and arching his back.

Peggy sighed. "I'll leave the door open, Patches, in case you change your mind."

Back in bed, before turning out the light, Peggy looked at the doorway. Patches still waited beyond, like a stiff, apprehensive sentinel.

CHAPTER SEVEN

The shrill ring of the telephone awakened Peggy. The clock on her night table read 8 a.m.

"It's for you, Peggy," her mother called. Peggy picked up her pink princess phone.

"Sorry to call so early."

"Julia?"

"Yes, it's me," Julia said. "I know we were supposed to get together this morning to do *you know what!*" The last words were spoken in a conspiratorial whisper. "But Mom's decided that we have to go into the city today for shopping and lunch."

Peggy blinked and came fully awake with a start. *She had forgotten about her appointment with Julia when she agreed to meet the other kids on the beach!*

"I'm sorry," Julia said.

"That's okay." *I'm the one who should be sorry,* Peggy thought.

"We're leaving early, so we'll probably be back by three or four. Can I come over then?"

"That would be great."

"See you later."

"Have fun in New York." Peggy hung up the phone and wondered how her plans with Julia had slipped her mind so completely. *I could have asked her to come along to the beach.* Even as she had that thought, however, Peggy knew that she would not have done so. She could not have said exactly why, but whatever the reason, it made her feel uncomfortable and guilty.

Why am I suddenly feeling guilty about so many things, Peggy wondered. *Would Doris Day feel guilty? Of course not!*

Forcing herself into positive movie star mode, Peggy strode to her dresser and pulled out her prettiest bathing suit. She was going to have a good time today with a bunch of great kids. And, although it took a lot of will power, she managed to avoid looking at THE CLOSET.

She arrived at the beach a few minutes before ten. She didn't see Sandra, but Kimberly was there, her golden mop pulled into a swinging ponytail. She was down near the water, standing with a group of other kids. The only other one Peggy recognized was Pete. As Peggy walked toward them, Kimberly turned around and saw her.

"Hey, everybody!" she announced. "Here's the new kid in town."

All eyes turned to Peggy. For a moment, she felt like a specimen in a zoo and wished she could disappear. Then she took a deep breath and approached the group.

Kimberly introduced the others. They had names like Harris, Ted, Anne, and Lana. Peggy couldn't remember which was which, but they greeted her with friendly remarks and smiles that made her feel better.

They were all going into seventh grade and began to discuss schedules, homerooms, and which teachers they either wanted or dreaded. At first, Peggy felt like a stupid outsider, but Pete and Kimberly tried to include her and give her advice on what to expect. Sandra arrived. As usual, she had the final word on every subject.

"I just don't want to get that *Mrs. Greenberg* for homeroom." Sandra emphasized the name with a sniff and a curl of the lip as though she were describing something nasty.

"Why not?" someone asked.

Sandra sneered. "She's so. . .so *ethnic*! My mother says that when she was a girl in this town they never hired *those people* as teachers."

"I heard that Mrs. Greenberg is nice," remarked one of the other girls. Peggy thought she was the one named Lana.

Sandra gave Lana a look that would have withered a rose. "You don't know what you're talking about!" she declared. Lana bit her lip and didn't say anything further.

Sandra kicked at an incoming wave. "Wait till you hear the latest!" she announced.

"What?" they all begged.

Sandra leaned forward and hissed. "You'll never guess who they hired to teach seventh grade science!"

"Who?"

Sandra crooked her finger, pulling the group closer. She looked around to make sure no one was nearby.

"A *colored guy,*" she whispered. "His name is Mr. Howard." She turned to Peggy. "My mother is on the School Board. That's how I know."

Peggy dug her toes into the wet sand and squirmed uncomfortably. She didn't like what she was hearing.

"But didn't your mother hire him?" she inquired. "I mean...being on the School Board and all?"

Sandra made a face. "Of course my mom didn't vote for him. She thinks that some of the new people on the Board must be Commies."

The boy they called Harris nodded. "Yesterday, I heard my dad say he doesn't like what's happening to this town." Harris was short and thick-necked, with muscular arms and chest.

"The wrong kinds of people are coming in," Sandra asserted. "Of course we don't mean you, Peggy," she added.

Peggy didn't know what to do or say. She sensed a nasty feeling in the air, and was thankful when Pete broke the tension by suggesting that they throw a ball around in the water. They splashed about, laughing and yelling, as though everyone had forgotten the words that had just been spoken. *Maybe they don't really mean anything bad*, Peggy told herself. After all, she was lucky to have already been accepted by kids in her class. She joined in the fun, but, somehow, her heart was not in it.

Finally, the group broke up and they all went their separate ways. Peggy headed for home, holding her sandals, with her beach towel slung over her shoulders. Her bare, wet feet slapped against the pavement, as she thought about her encounter with her new schoolmates.

"Peggy!"

Peggy pivoted around, and was surprised to see Pete running towards her. "I didn't know you were going this way, Pete," she remarked.

He shook his head. "I wasn't. I live in the other direction."

"Oh!" Peggy waited for Pete to explain. After a long, awkward silence he managed to blurt out a few words.

"You know. . .back there. . .what they said. . .I mean. . ." Pete looked around in all directions as if hoping to be rescued. He sighed and mumbled and scratched his head.

Peggy stared at him. *What was he trying to say?*

Pete shifted his feet uncomfortably and rolled his eyes upward as though looking for guidance from above. Finally, he blurted out quickly, "Don't mind Sandra. Sometimes she says...well...things."

"Do you agree with those things, Pete?"

He shrugged and spread out his hands. "Aw, that's just Sandra. It's all talk!"

Peggy noticed that Pete had been careful not to let on whether he agreed with Sandra or not, but Peggy didn't want to put him on the spot. He was nice to have come after her like this. "I'm glad you told me this, Pete," she said.

Pete's face eased into an expression of relief. His smile was warm and friendly. "Well, I'll see ya," he said, and loped off in the opposite direction.

"Bye." Peggy watched him for a while. Then she headed home.

Later that afternoon, she waited eagerly for Julia's arrival. Julia showed up about three-thirty, flaunting a new sky-blue poodle skirt and matching blouse.

"My Mom wanted me to save it for school,

but I just had to show you."

"It's fantastic!" Peggy pointed to the closet in the corner. "Are you ready?"

Julia hesitated. "I don't know. I've been thinking that maybe this is not such a good idea."

"But you're the one who insisted we go back!"

Julia shook her head. "I've got a bad feeling about it now."

"Julia! You promised!"

Julia sighed. "Okay, we might as well get it over with."

Peggy closed the door to her room. "My mom's in the sewing room," she explained. "I don't want her to hear."

"If there's anything to hear." It was clear from Julia's tone that she hoped nothing would happen. One part of Peggy agreed, but her hidden, more adventurous self almost wanted the opposite.

Peggy pushed the key into the lock and turned it. *Click!* "Are you ready?"

Julia nodded.

Taking a deep breath, Peggy opened the door. They stepped inside, and were immediately sucked into a dizzying windmill of whirling, stomach-turning turbulence that tossed them around like rag dolls. A moment later, the supernatural storm deposited them in the hidden room.

Back in time!

The first thing Peggy saw was Titus sitting on the bed. He looked a lot better. He had been cleaned up, and his ragged clothes exchanged for others that were old, but clean and whole. He was no longer trembling.

Peggy and Julia were seated on simple, wooden chairs facing the cot. Once more, they were clad in heavy, old-fashioned, long-skirted garments. Titus' eyes were fixed upon Julia.

"Be ye a runaway, too?" he asked.

Julia's jaw dropped. "Of course not!"

"Both girls are part of this household," came a voice from behind them. Peggy turned to see Mrs. Woodhouse standing near the door.

Titus' face shone with wonder as he pointed to Julia. "Be ye free then?"

Julia nodded.

Mrs. Woodhouse sat down next to Titus on

the cot. "Yes, Titus, she is free. Free the way God made her, the way He intended all His children to be." She smiled wearily. "We shall send you to freedom, too, as we have so many before."

Titus shook his head. "Glory be! Ah never knew ah could be so happy!"

"It's not over yet," Mrs. Woodhouse cautioned. "Many good folks like Josiah and his crew are working hard to help set your people free. But there are others. . . ." She frowned and a worried expression darkened her eyes.

"You mean the massas?" asked Titus.

The woman nodded. "Yes, the slave masters, and also the ones who care about nothing but earning a reward." She shook her head sadly. "I'm afraid there are several of these evil-doers plaguing our community at present."

Titus started in fright, and Mrs. Woodhouse tried to calm him with a pat on the arm. "Don't worry, Titus. I believe that you are safe here for the moment. The problem is that we may not be able to send you to the next station right away." She stood and smoothed the crisp white apron that was tied around her waist. "Josiah was hoping to take you there, but he has had to leave and go about his own business. It is dangerous now on the streets of Bay Point."

So they were still in Bay Point!

Titus looked at Mrs. Woodhouse hopelessly. "What will I do missus?"

"Nothing. We will care for you here until it is safe to leave and we can find another conductor."

Titus fell onto his knees beside the cot and took hold of Mrs. Whitehead's apron. "Oh, thankee, thankee."

Mrs. Whitehead reached down and pulled the boy to his feet. "Kneel only to God, Titus, not to me. We will put our trust in Him to carry you to freedom."

Titus stood, wiping tears from his eyes. "Amen," he added.

Peggy and Julia had been sitting as still as statues. Mrs. Whitehead turned to them. "You girls keep Titus company. I have work to do." She pulled out a small volume from her apron pocket, and handed it to Peggy. "You might read him some of this. I allow he surely hasn't heard of it where he has been, though it is famous in every state of this country and throughout the whole world."

Mrs. Whitehead went out. Peggy looked at the book. The title was on the cover, followed by the author's name. Uncle Tom's Cabin by Harriet Beecher Stowe.

"Have you read this book, Titus?" Peggy inquired.

He hung his head. "No'm. Ah never has learned my letters."

"Let's take turns reading it to him, Julia," Peggy suggested. Julia nodded.

The girls began reading the story of kindly Uncle Tom and his sufferings under the yoke of slavery.

"Tha's right! Tha's right!" Titus exclaimed from time to time. "Tha's surely how it be."

It was not a long book. By the time they reached the tragic ending, the girls were crying, and even Titus had to brush away a few tears.

"Oh, Titus!" Julia exclaimed. "How terrible it must have been for you!"

Just then, a commotion erupted downstairs. They could hear doors banging and the sound of rough, male voices.

Mrs. Whitehead rushed in. She was out of breath, fanning her face with a handkerchief. "Heaven help us!" she exclaimed. "The slave hunters are here."

CHAPTER EIGHT

"Oh Lawd," Titus moaned, "Don't send me back."

"No one is going to send you back if I have anything to say about it, Titus." Mrs. Woodhouse put her hand to her chest and sat down heavily on one of the chairs. "We've outwitted these evil men before." She frowned. "It's just that they never came storming into the house like this before."

The stamping and crashing sounds were getting louder. "They're going to the second floor now," said Mrs. Woodhouse. She stood up. "We must hurry. Titus, you stay here." She turned to Julia. "You, too, my dear."

"What?" Julia's eyes widened. "Why me?"

"It's your color, dear. These bounty hunters will seize any Negro, even those who are free, and then sell them. They will not spare you. You and Titus must remain here in the hiding place and not make a sound." She nodded to Peggy. "We will go out now and try to disguise the door to this room."

Peggy couldn't move. What if, like last time, she was whisked back to 1963 as soon as she left the room? Julia could be stuck here forever!

Peggy had a strong feeling that their time travel took place only in this room. *No*, she vowed silently, *I will not leave Julia here!*

Mrs. Woodhouse was at the doorway, her hand upon the knob. "Come!" she urged Peggy.

What can I do? Peggy wondered desperately. No matter what, she would not abandon her friend. She looked around desperately and her eyes lit upon the cot.

"I have a better idea," she told Mrs. Woodhouse.

"We have no time," the woman urged. "We must hide them now!"

"That's what I'm planning to do," Peggy told her. "Titus! Julia!" she called. "There's some space under the bed. Can you both fit in there?"

Quickly, Titus and Julia squeezed into the narrow opening on the floor beneath the cot.

"This is ridiculous," exclaimed Mrs. Woodhouse, wringing her handkerchief. "They can easily be seen."

"Not now." Peggy spread out one of the thin blankets so that it hung down to the floor, screening Julia and Titus.

"They'll just pull the covering off," Mrs. Woodhouse warned. "Oh, hurry. They are almost here!"

Peggy heard the heavy tread of boots upon the stairs. Quickly, she threw herself down on the bed and pulled the other blanket up to her neck. She let one arm dangle out limply. "Pretend I'm sick!" she whispered, just as the door to the room crashed open and two big men came in. They were mean looking brutes with cruel, hard faces, wearing long brown coats and thick leather boots.

"What's going on here?" demanded the taller of the two. He held up the long rifle he was carrying and pointed it straight at Peggy. "Who are you?" Her eyes were open just a slit, but enough to see the barrel of the gun. Her heart caught in her throat. It was all she could do not to jump up and run out at the speed of light back to the safety of nineteen hundred and sixty-three. Even with people building bomb shelters in their back yards, it was better than these terrible times!

"That is my niece," explained Mrs. Woodhouse in a quivering voice. "She is sick."

"So she's sick is she?" The man's eyes narrowed, and he advanced closer to the bed, still pointing the rifle at Peggy's head, threateningly. "What's wrong with her?" he sneered.

Peggy opened her eyes as though it took a great effort. "The pox," she said in a small, weak voice.

The men jumped back as though they had been struck.

Clever Mrs. Woodhouse caught on to Peggy's plan right away. "I'm keeping her up here in isolation," she told them. "No one but me goes near her."

"You better not be pulling anything funny on us!" the ruffian holding the rifle said, but both men looked frightened. They stomped from the room as though fleeing from a pack of devils. "We're not finished looking around this house," the bigger man warned Mrs. Woodhouse. "We'd best not find any Negroes here."

"Not in my house!" Mrs. Woodhouse assured him, as she closed the door.

For a few moments, the four people in that little room were as still and silent as statues. They could hear the slave hunters cursing loudly and clomping about, smashing and tossing boxes and furniture. Mrs. Woodhouse winced at the crash of breaking glass. "There's nothing I can do," she said sadly. "They think they have the right to do whatever they wish, and there is no one to prevent them."

Soon, they heard the men going down the stairs, and the sounds of destruction grew fainter until, at long last, the front door closed with an angry bang.

Mrs. Woodhouse sighed. "I think they are gone now," she whispered.

Peggy jumped off the bed while Titus and Julia crawled out from their hiding place beneath.

Mrs. Woodhouse seized Peggy's hand. "God bless you, my dear. The family is fortunate to have someone as committed and resourceful as you helping in our movement."

"Thank you." Peggy didn't feel that she was in any movement. "I just did what I could to help."

"And help you did!" Mrs. Woodhouse affirmed. She turned to Titus. "This girl has saved your life, Titus."

"Thankee." Titus' words were simple, but his eyes were moist with gratitude. "Ah'll never forget ye."

Mrs. Woodhouse opened the door. "I can use your help downstairs, girls. Say goodbye to Titus."

Peggy and Julia followed the woman out and were immediately back in their own world. Mrs. Woodhouse had disappeared, as had all signs of the bounty hunters' furious search. The room looked normal and welcoming, but was it? Peggy's nervous glance darted about the room suspiciously. Reality was no longer stable or trustworthy. The girls plopped down on Peggy's bed, confused and exhausted.

"Well," said Peggy. "I guess we weren't dreaming."

"No,"

"What are we going to do about it?" Peggy wondered.

"I don't know."

Peggy looked at her friend. Julia was usually so talkative, but she wasn't saying much now. Julia sat forward, her head hanging down and her shoulders slump. Her eyes seemed to be fixed on some unknown horror.

"Are you okay?" Peggy asked.

Julia raised her head and gazed at Peggy with a sadness so deep it made Peggy's heart ache.

"What is it?" Peggy begged.

"I could have gotten stuck in that time," Julia replied in a toneless voice.

"Me, too," Peggy agreed.

"It's not the same, Peggy. If those guys had caught me, they would have...I could have been forced to be a slave! For the rest of my life!" Julia's eyes suddenly filled up with tears.

Peggy put her arms around her friend and they hugged wordlessly. Then Julia broke away. "I am never, never going back into that room again!"

Peggy bit her lip. "Maybe it's time for me to tell my parents."

Julia swiped at her eyes with her hand. "They'll never believe you, girl."

Julia was right, of course. After dinner that evening, Peggy insisted that her parents examine the closet in her room. "There's something weird about it," she explained.

Later, Peggy was glad she had not told them more. Her parents went up to Peggy's room, opened the closet door, looked in, and remarked how nice it was to have a storage room so conveniently located.

That's all it was—an old, empty, musty room.

CHAPTER NINE

"That's all it was," Peggy told Julia on the phone the next morning, "an empty storage room."

"You went back there?" Julia sounded unbelieving.

"My mom and dad, too. Nothing happened." There was a brief silence on the other end. Then Julia murmured, "Maybe it's over."

"But why? Why should it be a time travel machine one day, and then just a really big closet the next?"

"I don't know," Julia admitted, "but there's one thing I know for sure."

"What?"

"I am never going there again. When I'm at

your house, girl, just keep that closet door shut."

"Okay." Peggy agreed, but in her heart she knew that it wasn't over for her. She would go back again, even if she had to do it alone.

Peggy got her mom's permission to go to the beach with Julia. She changed into her suit, and met Julia outside her house. A flock of raucous gulls flew overhead as the girls strolled toward the ocean.

"I'll bet the beach is crowded," Julia remarked. "Today's Friday, and that's when all the weekenders come.

Peggy's footsteps slowed. The words "crowded beach" made her think of Sandra and Pete and the other kids. She hoped they would not be there. Sandra had warned her about being seen with Julia.

"C'mon slowpoke," Julia urged. "You're walking as though your feet are made of wood."

Peggy quickened her pace, but she couldn't control the thoughts in her head that told her she had to ditch Julia to be part of Sandra's group. Yet Julia was Peggy's best friend in Bay Point–in more centuries than one. If only she could march up to Sandra, together with Julia, and say, *This is my friend.* That's what Doris Day would do.

When they arrived at the beach, Peggy was relieved to see that none of the kids were there. She was safe–at least for now!

They lay on their stomachs on the blanket, exposing their backs to a bright, hot sun in a vast, cloudless sky. "I've been doing a lot of thinking," Julia remarked, "about the things we saw in your closet."

"Yeah." Peggy nodded. "I wish I could stop thinking about those horrible men."

"Maybe it won't ever happen again," said Julia. "I mean going back in time."

Peggy propped herself up on one elbow. "What makes you say that?"

"It didn't happen when your parents went in."

"Perhaps it doesn't work with grownups," Peggy suggested.

Julia sat up suddenly. Her dark eyes glittered with sudden knowledge. "Or maybe we already did what we were meant to do."

"What we were meant to do?"

"Yeah. Maybe we were meant to save Titus. If we hadn't been there, those guys might have gotten him and sent him back to his master."

Peggy shook her head. "I don't know. It doesn't make sense."

"It makes as much sense as everything else. It's no weirder than believing in time travel."

"I don't believe in time travel," Peggy joked. Suddenly, she was aware that people nearby were staring at them. "Time travel," she yelled, and the curious faces turned quickly away. The girls looked at each other, and suddenly, the whole thing seemed hysterically funny in a crazy sort of way. They began laughing uncontrollably and raced to the water.

Later, when she was home alone in her room, Peggy replayed that conversation in her mind. Maybe Julia was right. Perhaps there would be no more time travel, now that Titus was safe.

But was he? They didn't know that. The slave hunters might have come back. Or Titus could have been caught on the way to the next station on the Underground Railroad. Peggy shook her head. No matter what Julia said or did, Peggy had to return one more time. Besides, Patches still refused to cross that threshold into Peggy's room.

"Mail for you, Peggy."

Peggy opened her door. Her mother was at the foot of the stairs waving an envelope. Peggy ran down and ripped it open.

"You are invited."

The card was from Sandra Bendix, asking Peggy to a pool party and barbecue at her house the next day.

"Can I go, Mom?"

"Of course."

"I have to RSVP."

"Okay. But Peggy?"

"What?" Peggy was eager to get to the phone.

"Do you think that Julia is invited, too?"

Peggy struggled to mask her feelings. She didn't want her mother to see the emotions that hurt and confused her. "I don't think so, Mom. She doesn't know Sandra."

CHAPTER TEN

At the party the next day Peggy tried to forget about Julia. At first, she had a good time. The kids she had met on the beach were there, along with a few others. They were friendly and wanted to know what it was like to live in "the old Deerfield place".

Sandra's family lived in a new, modern house with a big swimming pool and patio in the rear. Sandra's father wore a floppy chef's hat and a white apron with the words "World's Best Hamburger Maker" written across the front. He stayed in the background, grilling hamburgers and hot dogs for the kids.

Mrs. Bendix was more formidable. She was a

big woman, tall and broad-shouldered with blonde hair that was pulled back tightly into a severe bun. Her eyes had the same icy, blue penetrating gaze as Sandra's, and her voice was determined and sharp with authority.

Peggy thought she would be perfectly cast as a guard in a movie about a prison for women.

Mrs. Bendix peppered Peggy with questions. Where did they live before? What did her father do? Was he a college graduate? Was her mother? Who were her grandparents and where did they live?

Peggy answered as well as she could, but the steady inquisition made her nervous, and she felt small and insignificant under the woman's imperious stare. It was a relief when Peter finally came over and urged her into the pool.

Things went well after that for a while. There was a lot of friendly horseplay and laughing. But just as Peggy began to feel relaxed and comfortable, the atmosphere changed.

Peggy was seated at a large round patio table eating a hot dog and french fries. Sandra sat opposite, surrounded by Peter and some of the others.

"Were your parents upset," Sandra inquired,

"when they found out who was living next door?"

"No," Peggy replied truthfully.

A boy sitting opposite Peggy laughed. "Right!" he said in a mocking tone. "They don't mind it if their property value goes down." Peggy recognized the short, muscular guy she had met on the beach. She remembered that his name was Harris.

"We're all thrilled about our new neighbors. Right, guys?" added Harris.

"Right!" "Sure!" "You bet!" Others responded with obvious sarcasm.

"You poor thing," said Kimberly, shaking her golden curls. "You have to live right next door!"

I should say something, Peggy thought. I should tell them how nice the Purvises are. I should tell them that Julia is my best friend!

But she sat mute, chewing on her hot dog which was beginning to taste like dirty cardboard.

Sandra leaned forward. "Here's something not everyone knows yet."

"What?"

"My parents and some other decent people in town are forming a committee. They are going to make the Purvises move."

Harris snorted. "Yeah, right! They'll just tell them nicely to go away, and they'll leave." He got up and moved through the patio, looking around. Then he returned to his seat and whispered. "I got a better idea."

Peggy cringed. She was afraid to hear his "better idea".

"Anyway," Harris continued. "Me and a few others are going to pay those coloreds a visit soon. We'll show them that they aren't wanted here."

Peggy couldn't stand it any longer. She stood up, pushed back her chair, and made a big show of looking at the fish-shaped clock that hung on a nearby wall. "Oh!" she exclaimed. "I didn't know it was so late." She picked up her things and stuffed them into her tote bag, hoping no one had noticed the quiver in her voice.

"I'll walk you to the door, dear." Mrs. Bendix suddenly appeared at Peggy's side. "We're glad you could come." As Peggy left, she said, "I'll be in touch with your mother, soon. I hope you are *our kind of people.*"

Peggy ran all the way home. She didn't want to be the Bendix's kind of people.

CHAPTER ELEVEN

Peggy rushed into her house and slammed the door behind her. She leaned against the wall, out of breath. She had run all the way, desperate to reach the comfort and safety of home. But even now, she couldn't get rid of the cloud of nastiness that enveloped her as though she had been wallowing in the mud.

"Mom! Dad!" she called. She couldn't keep this experience to herself another minute. Her mother came down the stairs wearing new white capri pants and a red silk blouse that tied at the waist. Her dad followed, also dressed in going-out clothes.

"Peggy, we thought we'd be gone by the time

you got home," her mother exclaimed.

"Gone?"

"Don't you remember? Dad and I have been invited to dinner by his new boss and his wife."

Peggy couldn't think clearly. Her brain felt like a wad of cobwebs. "I guess I forgot," she admitted.

"We'll be back early," her dad said.

Peggy looked from one to the other. "But I have to talk to you. Now!"

Peggy's mom picked up her purse from the hall table. "Not now, dear. We're late already."

"But Mom...!"

"We'll talk when we get back." Peggy's mother gave her a hug, exclaiming. "And get out of that wet suit!"

"But Mom! Dad!"

"Later, Pumpkin." Her dad was already at the door. "We'll have a nice chat later."

Then they were gone.

Peggy sighed. *I have to warn the Purvises*, she thought as she went up to her room to change.

But what could she say to them? That someone was forming a committee? That a stupid, teenage boy was going to force them to move? It was ridiculous. She would feel like an idiot. But what if Harris meant what he said? What if he was planning something bad?

This was too much for her to handle alone. She would just wait until her parents got home and discuss it with them. They would know what to do.

Peggy tried to empty her mind. She got out her violin and music, set up the stand, and began to practice. Her mom had found a new violin teacher for her, recommended by Mrs. Purvis, but the teacher would be away for the rest of the summer. She had agreed to take Peggy on as a pupil in September. Meanwhile, Peggy had plenty of pieces and exercises to work on. She practiced for over an hour and, gradually, the magic of the music began to soothe her ragged nerves. For a short time, at least, she was able to forget that people such as Harris and the Bendixes existed.

Later, she went down to watch TV. Her parents had decided that the conservatory would be the TV room, so Peggy curled up on a new rattan couch with bright yellow and green cushions and tried to concentrate on "Mr. Ed".

Usually, she loved to sing along with the theme, "A horse is a horse, of course, of course," but this time, she couldn't summon the energy or the desire. Every time she heard the sound of a car, she jumped up and checked to see if her parents were home yet.

It seemed like forever. She looked at her watch. It was a quarter to ten. Surely, they'd be back any minute.

Just then, even over the sound of the TV, Peggy heard a loud crash, followed by another, and the sound of breaking glass. She rushed to the window in time to hear the revving of a souped-up engine, and see a car pulling away from in front of the house next door. There were four boys inside, all shouting, "Get out of town, coons!" One of them stuck his head out of the front passenger window and waved a fist threateningly.

The car roared past Peggy's house and down the street, but not before she had time to recognize the kid who had thrust out the fist.

It was Sandra's friend, Harris.

Peggy's heart pounded as she ran out the front door and looked next door. The Purvises had come out of their house and were standing on the front porch. Peggy rushed over.

Mr. Purvis was holding a rock with a note attached. He was a tall, thin, scholarly-looking man with gentle brown eyes behind large glasses. Julia had told Peggy that her father taught science at a nearby community college. He pointed to his living room window. "They threw this into the house," he exclaimed. Peggy could see that the window was shattered.

"Someone could have been hurt!" Mrs. Purvis was breathing heavily and clutching her chest with one hand.

By chance, Peggy's parents chose that moment to arrive home. They parked the car and joined Peggy and the Purvises. "What happened?" Peggy's dad asked.

Mr. Purvis showed them the rock. He read the note aloud. "This is your only warning. Get out of town before it's too late."

Peggy's dad headed for their house. "I'll phone the police," he said. Peggy sat down next to Julia, who had thrown herself onto a double swing at one end of the porch. Julia was shaking like a leaf in a windstorm. "Don't worry," said

Peggy, putting her arms around her friend. "They're just a bunch of stupid kids. The police will catch them."

"We didn't come outside in time to see who was in the car," said Julia. "Did you, Peggy?"

Peggy hesitated. If she told what she knew, Sandra and her pals would never talk to her again. Even worse, they might treat Peggy's family the way they were treating the Purvises.

Peggy shook her head, not able to speak the lie aloud.

"I'll bet it was Sandra," Julia groaned bitterly, her teeth still chattering. "I could tell right away that girl hated me."

Peggy was even more aware than Julia how Sandra and her family and friends felt about black people. But all she said was, "They were boys, and they looked older."

That was partially true. All the boys, except Harris, looked like high school students, and the guy at the wheel had to be old enough to drive a car.

Julia didn't accept that. "They're probably her friends. Or else. . ." She stood up, pulling out of Peggy's embrace. "Maybe no one in this town wants us here."

"Oh, no, Julia!" Peggy protested. "We love you, and I'll bet most people in Bay Point aren't prejudiced."

Julia shook her head. "You don't know that, Peggy."

Peggy had no answer. It was true that she didn't know how most people in this town felt, but the ones she had met had made their thoughts plain enough.

A screaming siren announced the arrival of the police as their car pulled to a halt in front of the Purvis' house. **BAY POINT POLICE DEPARTMENT** was emblazoned in large black letters across the side.

The police looked at the damage to the window. They examined the rock and the note, and placed them both in a bag as evidence. But they didn't offer much encouragement.

"It was probably just a prank," the older officer said. He was a big guy with a lined, weathered face that looked as though he spent most of his free time in the sun.

"A prank?" Mr. Purvis stared at the cop with disbelief. "You call this a prank?"

The policeman shrugged. "Well, you know

how kids are."

"No!" Mr. Purvis' anger was evident as he stepped close to the cop and faced him. "I don't know how kids are, or what kind of boys would do something like this!"

Mrs. Purvis pulled him back. "It's okay, Honey. I'm certain the officers will do their best to find those boys."

The cop's jaw was set grimly and his expression when he looked at the Purvises was not kind, but he said, "Sure, we'll look into it, but you know kids. They don't rat on one another."

The cops got into their car and drove off, leaving the two families standing on the porch, gazing at one another with disbelief.

Peggy's parents had a brief conversation with the Purvises and assured them of their support. "It's getting late," Peggy's mom then said. "We'd best get back to our own house."

Afterward, in the conservatory, they put on the eleven o'clock news, but no one really listened. Instead, they talked about what had just happened to the Purvises and discussed how they might be of help. Later, just before turning off the TV, Peggy's mom remarked. "Wasn't there something you wanted to tell us, Peggy?"

Peggy was wracked with confusion and guilt. She should have told the Purvises earlier. At least they would have been prepared, and they would have been able to give the cops some names.

On the other hand, who would have been blamed? Peggy, that's who! The whole town would turn against her. Even the cop had said that kids didn't rat on each other.

I don't want to be a rat, Peggy decided.

"Oh, it was nothing, really," she told her parents, as she yawned and said she was going to bed.

CHAPTER TWELVE

That night, Peggy had a disturbing dream. She was sitting on the cot in Mrs. Woodhouse's secret room, wearing the long, old-fashioned skirt. Her eyes were fixed on the closed door. She was waiting for someone or something. She did not know who or what, except that she was in danger. As time passed, she became more and more apprehensive. Fingers of fear traveled up her chest. Invisible claws scraped at her throat and she had to gasp for breath. She wanted to get up and flee but was unable to move, rooted to the spot, waiting helplessly for whatever terrible thing was about to happen. Her eyes darted about frantically. She peered into the shadowed corners of the small room, but no one was there. She was alone.

A sudden knock at the door startled her. It was more than a knock. It was a thunderous smash, as though someone had swung a gigantic ax against the wood, so loud and terrifying that she was flung up onto her feet like a puppet. It was followed by a second crash, and a booming voice roaring, "Open this door!"

Peggy tried to back up, to escape, but the cot was behind her and she had no place to go. Her ears rang with the third blow, which was accompanied by a loud splintering sound as the door fell apart. The big slave trader stood there, a rifle in one hand, an ax in the other.

"I've got you at last!" he bellowed, and strode toward Peggy. She lifted her arm for protection and was shocked to see that her skin was dark– darker than Julia's, almost as black as Titus. She examined her other arm, then lifted her skirt to look at her legs.

She was black, and the slave hunter had found her.

Rays of hatred shot from his inhuman eyes as he advanced upon her.

Panting to catch her breath, Peggy sat up in

her own bed. The morning sun twinkled through the slats of the window blinds. Her pulse was still racing as she examined her body, almost groaning aloud with relief to find that her skin had not changed color.

At that moment, Peggy understood perfectly why Julia would never go into the closet again.

The nightmare was so vivid that it bothered her for hours. She watched workmen arrive next door and begin to repair the damage done to the Purvis' window, and that made her even more anxious. Later that morning, she went for a walk with Julia and told her about the dream.

Julia nodded. "Well, that's it," she said.

"What?"

"It's a warning that you shouldn't go into that room again."

"It's just a dream, Julia."

Julia stopped and seized Peggy's arm. "Dreams can tell us things," she insisted. "It's a sign. Don't go there again."

Peggy smiled. Julia was so intense!

"Don't laugh at me!" Peggy had never heard her friend sound so serious. "Promise me you won't time-travel again."

Peggy pulled away. "I can't do that." They had stopped in front of a small gift shop, and she stared at the shells and tee shirts and other souvenirs in the window.

"But Peggy. . ." Julia was interrupted by a new arrival.

"Hi, Peggy," said Peter.

She hadn't seen him approaching. He was smiling, and looking at Julia.

"Hi, Peter." Peggy hesitated, and then plunged ahead. "This is my friend, Julia."

Peter nodded at Julia. "Hi."

They talked about the weather and where they were going. "I'm headed for the hardware store," Peter told them. "My mom needs some light bulbs." He looked from one girl to the other. "Wanna come along?"

"Sure." They walked on companionably. Finally, Peter spoke about the thing that was on all their minds. "I. . .um. . .I heard about what happened at your house last night," he told Julia.

"I guess the whole town knows about it now."

Peter nodded. "That's for sure. I. . .well. . .I just wanted to tell you that I'm sorry. It was rotten."

"Thanks." They reached the hardware store and said goodbye. Peter started to open the door, then turned around and bent close to Julia.

"You should be careful," he said, his eyes darting nervously from side to side as though he was afraid of being overheard.

"What do you mean?"

"Just be careful. That's all." A group of shoppers appeared from around the corner, and Peter disappeared like a shot into the store. The girls stared after him.

"What was that all about?" Julia asked.

Peggy shook her head. "I don't know. I guess he's just worried about you after what happened last night."

"He seems like a nice guy," Julia murmured. "Too bad the other people in this town aren't like him."

"Maybe they are," Peggy said, but Julia looked doubtful. Peggy shared her friend's doubts. Peter's words "You should be careful" rang in her head like a warning bell, but she tried to brush away the sounds for Julia's sake. Maybe it didn't mean anything, she told herself.

Julia had lunch at Peggy's house. They didn't want to disturb Peggy's mom, who was in the sewing room working on slipcovers for their new couch, so they slapped together some peanut butter and jelly sandwiches. They had demolished the sandwiches and were trying to decide on Twinkies or Oreos for dessert when the phone rang. It was Julia's mother. Peggy handed her the phone. A long conversation followed. When Julia hung up, she turned to Peggy, her dark eyes shining.

"You'll never guess where we're going."

"Where?"

"Washington."

"Washington, DC?" asked Peggy. "But why?"

"Dr. King is marching," Julia explained. "And we're going down there to march with him."

Peggy knew that Martin Luther King was a leader in the civil rights movement. She had seen him on television a few months earlier. He had been in Birmingham, Alabama leading a campaign to help black people register to vote and get other rights. The police set vicious dogs upon the demonstrators and turned high-pressure fire hoses on them. Peggy would never forget the sight of hundreds of teenagers and children singing one minute and the next being attacked by huge dogs and pinned to buildings by torrents of water. And only recently, a white group had placed dynamite in a black church in Alabama. It was terrible. Four children had been killed in the explosion. Peggy remembered Dr. King and his passionate call for justice.

"This will be the biggest freedom march in history," Julia continued. "My mother said there will be four busloads of people just from our old church in New York. That's where we are going to board the 'freedom bus.'" Julia sat down and bit into a cookie. "I can't believe we're really going!" she exclaimed.

Peggy shook her head. "I still don't understand."

"How can you say that?" Julia jumped up. "You know how the people here are treating my family! You saw that rock they threw last night!"

Peggy remembered. "Yes, it was awful."

"It's ten times worse in the South. Don't you think something needs to be done?" Julia demanded.

Peggy nodded. Fragments of her horrible

dream came back to her. She had felt what it was like to have black skin, to be a target of someone's hate.

"My mom said that thousands of people are going–hundreds of thousands. They're coming from everywhere in the country on 'freedom buses' and 'freedom trains'. We want freedom and equal rights."

"And will this Dr. King be able to get that for you?" Peggy asked.

Julia's voice exploded with hope. "You bet!" Her big grin was filled with such delight that Peggy could not help but smile too. "So when are you going?" she asked.

"Soon." Julia looked up at a big calendar that hung on the wall. "August 28th–that's only three days off."

The phone rang again. "It's my mother," exclaimed Julia. "She said she would call again with more details." She rushed over to pick up the phone. "Hello, Mom? What? Oh!" Julia made a face and handed the receiver to Peggy. "It's your friend!"

"Hello?"

Sandra's voice at the other end was sharp

and clear. "Who answered the phone? It's the colored girl, isn't it?"

"Um..m..m." Peggy couldn't think what to say. But it didn't matter. Sandra rushed ahead.

"I can't believe this! Don't you want to be friends with the kids in town?"

"Yes," Peggy murmured.

"Well, you're not going to fit in if you keep hanging out with that undesirable element. Do you understand?"

"But..."

"No 'buts'," Sandra insisted. "I was calling to see if you wanted to meet us on the beach this afternoon. But don't bother coming. No one will talk to you if you do. You have to make up your mind, do you hear? You can't have it both ways. It's either them or us!"

CHAPTER THIRTEEN

The next few days were the worst of Peggy's life. The new school term would be starting in just a couple of weeks. *Junior High School!* Peggy wanted so much to fit in with the other kids, to have lots of friends, to go to parties, to talk for hours on the phone. But they wouldn't let her do that unless she was ready to betray the friend she already had. She liked Julia a lot. It felt as if they had been pals for a long time. Besides, the town was treating the Purvises unfairly. It was only right to stand by them.

But how she yearned to be part of the crowd! Peggy felt as though she were being pulled in two opposing directions and torn apart. What could she do?

She chose to avoid making any decision by not leaving her room. She pretended to be sick and stayed in bed. *I'm such a coward and a phony*, she thought as her mother rushed up and down the stairs to take her temperature and bring her cool drinks and meals on a tray.

Julia called every few hours, but Peggy said she was too sick to talk on the phone. She read. She listened to music. She watched a small TV that her father brought up to her room. She tried not to think about Julia. She tried not to think about Sandra. Most of all, she tried not to look at the closet in the far corner that seemed to call to her with a mysterious force.

As each day came to a close, she crossed it off with a large X on the "Teen Fashion Calendar of 1963" that hung above her desk. The August girl had red gold hair pulled back into a high, swingy pony tail. She wore tight-fitting blue jeans, a white tee shirt, and white tennis shoes. Each time Peggy drew the X, she thought, *That's one less day to worry about.* Maybe something would happen that would make the decision for her.

On the evening of the second day of her self-imposed isolation, Peggy was watching *The Dick Van Dyke Show* when her mother came in. "Pick up your phone," she told Peggy. "Julia wants to talk to you."

Peggy managed to force out a few pathetic coughs. "I don't feel well enough."

"She's calling to say goodbye, Peggy. The Purvises are going to Washington tomorrow." Peggy's mom spoke in a tone of voice she didn't use very often.

Peggy picked up her princess phone. "Hi, Julia."

"How are you feeling?"

Peggy managed a cough. "A little better."

"I wanted to see you, but Mom wouldn't let me. She said you might have something contagious."

An unpleasant feeling of guilt crept over Peggy like a coat that was too tight. Would Julia care about her as much if she knew how disloyal Peggy had been? She suddenly felt as sick as she had been pretending to be.

Julia was still chattering excitedly into the phone. "We're leaving early tomorrow morning. It's going to be so wonderful, Peggy. Imagine.

Going to Washington and marching with Dr. King!"

"That's great, Julia."

"It's all going to be on TV. You'll watch, won't you?"

"Sure."

"Look for me," said Julia. "I'm going to wear my new poodle skirt. I'll be the coolest cat there."

"I'll look for you." Peggy almost envied Julia her excitement and joy. "Have a great time."

"Okay, girl. See you when I get back! And you get all better, okay?"

"Okay."

Peggy put down the phone. Her mother was still standing at the door, looking at her curiously. "You didn't sound very enthusiastic," she remarked.

"I don't feel well," Peggy wailed and threw herself down on the pillow.

The next morning, Peggy decided it was time to get up and face the world. She put on a Beach Boys record while she took a shower and got dressed. Then, she went down to breakfast for the first time in days.

Her Mom and Dad were so happy to see she

was better that Peggy felt even guiltier. Her Dad was just leaving for work. He planted a loud kiss on her forehead. "Glad to have you back, Pumpkin."

Peggy plunked herself down at the kitchen table and dove into a big stack of pancakes. Her Mom was delighted and sat opposite with a mug of coffee. "It was still dark when the Purvises left," she told Peggy. "I was already up and saw them from the window."

"They have a long trip," Peggy murmured as she poured on more syrup.

"It's wonderful to have a cause to believe in," Peggy's mom remarked. "I hope this march does some good."

"Me, too." Peggy understood racial problems even better than her mother did. In a sense, she had lived them herself! The image of Titus came into her mind. Once again, she saw the terror in his eyes and realized the suffering he had endured as a slave. What had happened to Titus? Had he gotten away safely? Or had the slave hunters caught him? Julia had said she believed that their journey through time had been for the purpose of saving Titus, and that mission had been accomplished. But they couldn't know that for sure. They had to go back one more time to find out. Julia was too scared to do it, so it was up to Peggy to go alone.

"Peggy?" She realized that her mother was talking to her. "Are you sure you're feeling okay?" her Mom asked. "Maybe it's too soon to be eating pancakes."

"No way!" Peggy told her, piling a few more onto her plate, then dousing them with syrup. "I'm fine!" Peggy knew what she had to do now. It was as though she had been struggling through a blinding storm and had suddenly come out on the other side, where everything was sharp and clear. She would go into the closet one more time to find out what had happened to Titus. That was it! One more trip into the past. Then she would know what she had to do next. Maybe this didn't make much sense, but it just seemed right somehow.

A few hours later, Peggy was in her room, staring at *the closet*, trying to work up the courage to enter one more time. "What do you think, Patches?" she asked. "Should I go in there?"

Patches didn't respond. He was stretched

across the doorway to Peggy's room, silent and unmoving as a lump of coal. Only his tail twitched to express his displeasure. He still refused to enter, but was obviously annoyed not to be able to do so.

"I'll do it!" Peggy told the cat, and started toward the closet. She was just about to open the door when her mother called from below.

"Hurry, Peggy. The March is on TV."

"Buses have been arriving for hours," Peggy's mother announced when Peggy came down. "There are a hundred thousand people already, and hundreds of thousands more are expected before the day is over."

Peggy stared at the incredible sight on the screen. She had never seen such huge crowds. There were all sorts of people–black and white, young and old, some well dressed and others wearing shabby clothes. Many of them carried signs. *"Freedom Now,"* said one. Another called for *"Jobs for Every American."* A young black woman wearing a paisley dress waved a sign reading, *"We Must Be Accorded Full Rights as Americans Not In the Future But Now."* A white man held up a sign protesting lynching. *"Stop*

Legal Murders", it demanded.

Peggy recognized the Washington Monument in the background. A stage had been set up and someone was performing a song. It was Bob Dylan's *Blowin' in the Wind*. The camera closed in on the singer and Peggy squealed. "It's Bob Dylan himself!"

Her Mom nodded. "You missed Joan Baez," she informed Peggy.

"What did she sing?"

"*We Shall Overcome*. And everyone sang along. It was inspiring."

They stayed glued to the set. Other entertainers came along and the crowds grew larger and larger. Peggy peered at the screen, searching for the Purvises, but it was impossible–there were too many people. The Gormans watched as throngs began to march up Independence and Constitution Avenues to the Lincoln Memorial. Another stage had been put in front of the beautiful white marble columns with the massive figure of Abraham Lincoln visible inside.

The speeches began. Peggy expected to be bored, but the messages were so exciting. Besides, she recognized many well-known actors and actresses. There was Charlton Heston, Marlon Brando, and Paul Newman, who Peggy thought was the handsomest man alive. A small, neatly-dressed woman named Rosa Parks was wildly applauded, and Peggy's mother explained that Rosa Parks had bravely refused to move to the rear of a bus, where blacks were expected to ride, and had taken a seat in front because it was the only one available. It seemed such a small thing, Peggy thought, but evidently had caused a huge fuss.

Peggy's mom identified the civil rights leaders as they came onto the podium. There was Roy Wilkins, president of the National Association for the Advancement of Colored People, and John Lewis who made a passionate plea for jobs and equality.

Peggy's father arrived home early and joined them. "I don't want to miss this," he explained. "I know it will go down in history." They even ate in front of the TV from trays of food Peggy's mom prepared.

A large black woman with an even bigger voice sang a song called, *I've Been 'Buked and I've Been Scorned*. "That's the gospel singer,

Mahalia Jackson," Peggy's mom whispered.

Peggy stood up to stretch her legs. She strolled over to the window. The sun was beginning to set behind dense clouds, and the light dimmed as dusk began to fall. Peggy noticed movement in the bushes between their house and the Purvis'. She peered out and saw several figures there in the shadows. Suddenly, the clouds parted for just a few seconds and a glimmer of sunlight fell on the area. She recognized Harris and his friends. What were they up to? She was about to say something to her parents, when her father called to her.

"Come back," he said urgently, "The main speaker is about to begin."

Then Dr. Martin Luther King stepped up to the podium and a deep silence fell over the huge crowd. Peggy was surprised at Dr. King's appearance. She had heard him described as a great civil rights leader, and expected someone large and imposing. King was an ordinary looking man of medium height with a mild, pleasant manner. But when he began to speak, it soon became apparent that there was nothing ordinary about this man.

"I am happy to join you today," he began, "in what will go down in history as the greatest demonstration for freedom in the history of our nation." His voice was deep and melodious. Abraham Lincoln in the background seemed to be listening as Dr. King sadly described how, one hundred years after the Emancipation Proclamation, black people were still not free, "crippled by the manacles of segregation and the chains of discrimination." He spoke of the promise of America to guarantee everyone the right to life, liberty and the pursuit of happiness as stated in the Declaration of Independence. "Now is the time to make real the promises of democracy," he said. "Now is the time to make justice a reality for all God's children."

Peggy watched the uplifted faces of the demonstrators, their eyes fastened upon the speaker with longing and hope. Peggy felt as though he was talking directly to her. Even her parents, who usually commented non-stop on anything they saw on TV, watched in silence as Dr. King called for change through non-violent means. His voice rose in a passionate crescendo and people in the crowd responded with cries of approval.

"I have a dream," Dr. King told them and all of America. "I have a dream that one day on the red hills of Georgia, sons of former slaves and sons of former slave-owners will be able to sit down together at the table of brotherhood." The crowd roared. "I have a dream," he continued, "my four little children will one day live in a nation where they will not be judged by the color of their skin but by the content of their character." Then he concluded in ringing tones. "When we allow freedom to ring from every state and every city, we will be able to speed up that day when all God's children will be able to join hands and sing in the words of the old Negro spiritual: 'Free at last! Free at last! Thank God almighty we are free at last.'"

Dr. King's words pierced Peggy's heart like a knife. She remembered how she had listened timidly as Sandra and her friends spit out words of hatred and bigotry, and she felt ashamed. It would be different in the future, Peggy vowed silently. Never again would she be silent in the face of prejudice and evil. She would be loyal to her friend and stand up for what was right.

"Peggy?" Her father was talking to her.

"Yes?"

"Were you listening to Martin Luther King?"

"Yes."

"Remember his words." Her dad's voice was serious. "They will surely go down in history."

"Yes, Dad, I. . ."

Peggy's mother interrupted. "What's that smell?"

They all jumped up and looked around, sniffing. "It smells like smoke," said Peggy's dad. "I think it's coming from outside." He strode to the front door and opened it. Peggy and her mother followed.

"The Purvis' house!" Mr. Gorman exclaimed. "It's on fire!"

CHAPTER FOURTEEN

Smoke was coming from the Purvis house.

"I'll call the fire department!" Mrs. Gorman ran back into the house.

Peggy and her father hurried to get a better look. Tongues of flame were creeping up the side and front of the building.

"I hope there's no one inside," said a blonde woman wearing white shorts and a blue striped tee shirt. She was standing on the sidewalk with a small white dog at her side that was tugging on its leash. She turned to Mr. Gorman. "Somebody should get help."

Peggy's father nodded. "The family isn't home. My wife is calling the fire department."

Peggy was too shocked to speak. The fire seemed to be growing stronger every second. Red and yellow flames were spreading and shooting up toward the roof. The air filled with the stench of smoke and the crackling of fire.

More people began to appear on the sidewalk.

"Someone might be inside!" A tall, white-haired man headed for the front porch. Peggy's father pulled him back. "The family is away," he informed the would-be hero. "And the firemen should be here any minute."

A woman in the gathering crowd screamed when the air was suddenly rent by the crash of smashing glass as the pressure of the blaze caused windows to break. The glow of the fire showed curtains and furniture smoldering and burning. Peggy felt a pang of pain as she remembered how proud and pleased Mrs. Purvis had been about her recently decorated home.

Pieces of the roof began to crumble and break off, causing sparks of fire to scatter into the air.

Peggy's mother seized her husband's arm. "That's awfully close to our house," she said in a worried voice.

"What's taking the firemen so long?" someone in the crowd complained.

"How could this have started?" The woman with the little dog shook her head in disbelief.

Peggy thought of the boys she had seen lurking in the bushes. The threats she had heard at Sandra's party cut into her memory like a knife. *We'll show them they aren't wanted here.* "Dad," she said, "I think I know….."

She was interrupted by the shriek of sirens. Two fire engines roared down the street and came to a screeching stop in front of the burning house, followed by a police car with the words **"CHIEF**, and **BAY POINT POLICE DEPARTMENT"** emblazoned on the door. The firemen charged out of their trucks, pulled out the fire hoses, quickly attached them to a hydrant and began to train streams of water upon the fire.

Peggy's mother pointed to their own house. "Look!" she shouted.

Burning embers from the fire next door had landed on one side of the Gorman's house. The wooden shingles ignited quickly and began to flicker, then burst into flame on the roof and third floor.

That's my room! Peggy realized in horror.

Peggy's father rushed over to one of the firefighters and pointed to the spreading fire. Quickly, the man moved one of the hoses toward it.

It took several minutes to control that part of the blaze and keep it from reaching the lower floors, but not before that corner of the house had become blackened and charred.

Meanwhile, the fire at the Purvis' continued to sputter and flare up for at least half an hour more before the firefighters succeeded in putting it out. Peggy's mom tried to enter her own house, but a firefighter pulled her back. "Best wait a while, ma'am," he cautioned.

"Where are the people who live here?" A burly, middle-aged man in a police uniform had gotten out of the patrol car, followed by two younger police officers. The one in charge wore a cap with the word *CHIEF* on the front. He had thick black hair, beady, close-set eyes, and a ruddy complexion.

Peggy's dad stepped up. "The Purvises are out of town."

"Purvis?" The chief's eyes narrowed. "Seems I've heard that name before." Peggy did not like the tone of his voice. There was something familiar about the man, even though she was sure she had never seen him before.

Peggy pulled her father aside. "Dad," she said urgently. "I might know who started this fire." He turned to her in surprise. "What do you mean?" She had his full attention now, and told him about the boys she had seen earlier lurking in the bushes.

"You have to tell the police," he said.

None of the kids will ever talk to me again, Peggy thought. Then she remembered Martin Luther King's stirring message, and knew that she had to do what was right. She and her dad went over to the Chief.

They introduced themselves. "I'm Jim Gorman and this is my daughter, Peggy. We live next door."

The chief eyed them suspiciously. "Chief Wilkerson here. Harris Wilkerson, Senior."

"Do the firefighters have any idea how the fire started?" Peggy's dad asked.

"There are signs it might be arson."

"My daughter might know something about that." He pushed Peggy forward. "Tell the Chief what you saw."

Peggy stared at the big policeman and the words stuck in her throat. *Harris Wilkerson Senior? Harris,* like Sandra's friend? Peggy had never heard Harris' last name, but she now suspected it was Wilkerson. That's why the Chief had seemed familiar. He must be Harris' father!

"Well?" he asked, staring at her sternly. "What do you think you saw?"

"Some boys in the bushes," Peggy whispered.

"Speak up!" he demanded in an angry tone.

"I saw three boys hiding in the bushes between our houses a little while before the fire started," she told him.

"Did you recognize any of them?"

Peggy nodded. "One of them. I met him at the Bendix's house. His name is … er…" She was almost paralyzed with fear but somehow managed to croak out the rest of the sentence. "Harris."

The chief's face turned as red and angry as the roaring fire had been. "How could you know that at night?" he demanded.

"It wasn't dark yet when I saw them."

"Listen, you little...." Chief Wilkerson paused when he noticed that a group of people had gathered around them and were listening. He pulled a notebook out of his pocket and wrote something down. "What is this kid's last name?" he asked, barely hiding his fury.

Peggy shrugged. "I don't know."

The Chief put his notebook away and glanced at the crowd. "I'll look into this," he announced, then waved to the other cops. They got back into their patrol car and sped off.

Peggy and her dad exchanged glances.

"I think one of those boys is the Chief's son," she told him. "They'll surely get away with it now."

CHAPTER FIFTEEN

Much later that night, Peggy and her parents watched a cab pull to a halt in front of the house next door. The taxi doors opened and the Purvises climbed out. They stared in horror and disbelief at the smoky, blackened shell of what had once been their beautiful home. Peggy rushed to throw trembling arms around her friend. "It's all my fault!" she sobbed, while her parents explained to the dazed Purvises what had happened.

"You'll stay with us for a while," Peggy's mom insisted. Fortunately, the fire had damaged only the roof and one corner of their third floor, unlike the Purvis' house, which was a mess. The firemen had said it was too dangerous for them to go in immediately.

Peggy's brain felt as if it was encased in a black fog. Everything that had happened during the past twenty-four hours seemed unreal. Watching the March on Washington on TV had been like nothing she had ever experienced before. All those people gathering peacefully in their quest for equality and civil rights! She could only imagine what it must have been like to actually be there.

And then the fire! Peggy had seen burning buildings in the movies or on TV but the reality was totally different and far more terrifying. The leaping flames that ripped and roared like a devouring monster. The stench of burning wood, smoke, and ashes clung to her nose, her throat, and even her clothes. Worst of all, though, was Peggy's sickening sense of guilt. She had seen those boys hanging out there. She should have realized they were up to no good. Why hadn't she told someone about it?

"It's my fault," Peggy sobbed again.

"It's not your fault," Julia insisted, but Peggy couldn't shake a choking sense of guilt.

Peggy had been worried about her room, but most of it was untouched. Only one corner had been affected–the corner that contained the mysterious closet. The closet door had fallen off and there was nothing inside but charred walls and blackened ceiling.

There wasn't much sleep for anyone that night. The Purvises were confused and nervous. Mrs. Purvis seemed unable to keep back bursts of tears. "My home, my lovely home," she moaned.

Mr. Purvis alternated between despair and anger. He held his head in his hands saying, "What are we going to do? What are we going to do?" The next moment, he paced the floor in a rage, shouting about "those stupid racists." The Gormans tried to comfort their neighbors and Peggy's mom made pots of tea and hot cocoa.

Peggy and Julia went up to Peggy's room. No one insisted that they go to sleep, and they had no intention of doing so. Peggy took out two pairs of pajamas. They put them on and curled up on the shag rug.

"My clothes must be ruined!" Julia moaned. "I'll have nothing to wear to school."

"You can borrow mine," Peggy assured her.

"Besides, school won't begin for two weeks. You'll have plenty of time to buy new ones."

Julia frowned. "I don't know why I'm worried about school," she said. "We may not even be living here by then."

Peggy looked at her in surprise. "What do you mean? I'm sure your house can be fixed up."

"I mean," said Julia tightly, "that we might not be able to stay in Bay Point."

"Why not?"

"It is obvious, isn't it, that we are not wanted here."

Peggy had never seen such a hard look on Julia's face before. She didn't know what to say, so she went over to the record player and put on a Beach Boys record. Maybe the music would improve Julia's mood. Peggy sat down again and took Julia's hand as the sounds of *Surfin' U.S.A.* washed over them. "I want you here," she told her friend.

Julia pulled away. "That's not enough," she said. "How can we stay in a place where everyone hates us?"

"You're wrong, Julia!" Peggy insisted. "Sure, there are some horrible people here, but I'll bet there are lots of nice ones, too."

Julia pointed to the blackened closet in the far corner. "Remember Titus?" she asked. "I really understand now the way he must have felt."

"He was a slave! And he was on his way to freedom," Peggy pointed out, picturing Titus and how hopeful he had been when they saw him last. She jumped up and ran over to the closet that had been their time machine. Julia followed, sniffing the air. "It smells smoky in this part of the room," she remarked. "Like a fireplace when there are only hot ashes left."

They peered into the remains of the closet. The walls and ceiling were sooty and there were sprinklings of ashes on the floor. . "Julia," Peggy whispered, "Now we'll never be able to find out what happened to Titus."

"Or Mrs. Whitehead," Julia added, looking thoughtful. "She was a good person."

"There are good folks around today, too," Peggy insisted, but Julia's expression was tight and unconvinced. She seemed more comfortable talking about the past. "I know I said I would never go back," Julia said, "but now I can't help but wonder about those people."

"I think you were right in what you said before," said Peggy.

"What was that?"

"You said that there was a purpose to our trip back in time—that it was to save Titus, and that's what we did."

A ghost of a smile flitted over Julia's lips. "We did that, didn't we? You came up with a super plan to fool the slave hunters."

Peggy nodded. "It worked anyway. And I gave myself a comfortable position on the bed. Not squished underneath like you were."

"It wasn't so bad to be pushed up against Titus." A devilish gleam came into Julia's dark eyes and she looked once again like the Julia before all the bad stuff happened. "He was kind of cute, don't you think?"

"Julia!" Peggy yelled, and they both burst into laughter. They talked on and on about their weird experiences in the closet. About the strange, uncomfortable clothes they were wearing. About Mrs. Whitehead and the fisherman, who were members of the Underground Railroad. About the scary, evil slave hunters. But most of all about Titus, and their longing to know whether or not he had finally reached safety. For a while, Julia seemed to forget her current problems.

Finally, they ran out of words and sat in silence, lost in memories of their travels through time, as they listened to the final song on the Beach Boys record. "I said yes, I said," sang Brian Wilson, "Finders keepers, losers weepers."

Hours later, they finally fell into an exhausted sleep. When they woke the next morning, the sun streaked into the room as cheerfully as though nothing bad had happened.

"What's that noise?" Peggy wondered aloud. She looked at the clock on her night table. "Wow! Did we sleep late! It's almost eleven o'clock."

Julia rubbed her eyes. "I hear voices and hammering."

Suddenly wide-awake, the girls jumped out of bed like two bullets shot from a gun, and rushed to look out the window.

Julia's mother and father were standing on the sidewalk looking up at the sad remains of their house. The outside walls were all standing, although shingles had fallen off or were hanging in crazy angles. Some of the windows were blackened and too coated with soot to see inside. One of the steps that led up to the front porch was gone and the porch floor was broken and uneven.

But the most amazing thing was happening on and near the porch. Six or seven men were hard at work sawing and hammering, taking up the old floor and replacing it with a new one. Dozens more men and women were on the sidewalk gathered around the Purvises. Some of them were holding boxes or packages.

"I've got to see this!" shouted Julia.

"Me, too!"

They brushed their teeth quickly, rushed through their showers and threw on some clothes. Peggy insisted that Julia borrow a pair of brand new khaki shorts. They hurried downstairs and found an empty house, then ran outside.

Julia rushed over to join her parents. Peggy was about to follow when she heard her Dad's voice. He said "Peggy" softly, and she realized that her parents were sitting on the porch. She joined them and sat down on a two-seater swinging chair that the previous owners had left behind. "What's going on next door?" Peggy asked.

"The good folks of Bay Point are making themselves known," he replied.

"What do you mean?"

"The word seems to have gotten out about what happened to the Purvises," her father explained. "People have been coming by all morning."

"Who are those guys fixing the porch?"

"Just neighbors," said Mrs. Gorman, "trying to be of help. Your father was working there for the past two hours, too. I insisted he take a little rest."

Peggy jumped up and ran to the end of the porch where she had a better view. The crowd around the Purvises had grown larger. People were pushing forward to shake their hands. She couldn't hear most of what was being said, but one man spoke in a booming voice. "Please don't judge this town by the actions of a fanatical few," he said.

A feeling of joy seized Peggy's heart like a burst of light. She had feared that everyone in Bay Point was like Sandra and her friends, but now she could see that was not true. She turned to her parents. "What's going to happen now?"

"Thank God they've got insurance," Peggy's mom said. "That will cover the cost of rebuilding the house."

"Where will they live in the meantime?"
"We invited them to stay here. In fact, a number of people have offered to share their homes, but the Purvises decided to stay at a nearby motel until the work is finished. The insurance covers that expense, too."

Julia came rushing up. "Did you see them?" she shouted. "Did you see all those people?"
Peggy nodded.

"They're on our side!" Julia exclaimed. "I can hardly believe it."

Peggy plopped down on the swing again. Julia joined her and they pushed back and forth together. "I guess you won't be leaving Bay Point," said Peggy.

Julia shook her head. "No way! Bay Point is looking better than ever. Even my parents are amazed at the way people have spoken up for us."

But Peggy knew that not everyone was on the Purvis' side. "Have the cops been by?" she asked her father.

"I haven't seen them."

Peggy frowned. "Shouldn't they be investigating the fire?"

Mr. Gorman shrugged. "I'm sure they are looking into it."

"Are they?" Peggy wasn't so sure. Not after the way Chief Wilkerson had acted. She squeezed Julia's hand. "I know Harris and his pals did this, Julia. I saw them there that night, and they won't get away with it. I promise!"

CHAPTER SIXTEEN

Peggy didn't usually read newspapers. But she was the first one to grab the *Bay Point Gazette* when it arrived that afternoon. She had expected to see a big article about the fire on the front page. Instead she discovered the story at the bottom of page four. *Fire on Blount Street,* said the small headline, and underneath. "Cause of blaze under investigation."

I'll bet! Peggy fumed to herself.

The Purvises had checked into their motel and then gone shopping for new clothes. Peggy sat alone in her room and pondered the problem. It didn't seem likely that the police would really investigate. Not if the Chief was Harris' father! She had promised Julia that the boys who set the fire would not get away with it, but what could she do?

Peggy felt something soft and furry rub against her leg.

"Patches!" she cried in delight. The cat had finally decided to enter Peggy's room. Peggy looked at the burned out closet in the corner. "I guess this means that the past is gone forever," she told the cat. Patches mewed in agreement and curled up on the bed next to Peggy. *It's just as well,* Peggy thought to herself. *I have a big problem to solve right here in the present.*

But hadn't she solved an even bigger problem in that room from the past? Hadn't she saved Titus from the slave hunters? Surely she should be able to think of something to do now! But what? She stared again at the article in the newspaper.

Newspaper! That was it! Peggy jumped off the bed, disturbing Patches who hissed in protest. Peggy ignored him and checked out the newspaper again. There were two things she needed–the name of the person who wrote the article and the address of the newspaper. These were easy to find. The reporter's name was A. Flaherty. The newspaper office was on Bayview Road. That was only a few blocks from Peggy's house. Actually, Bay Point was such a small community that nothing was a great distance from any other place in town.

Excited and filled with energy now that she had a plan, Peggy rushed down the stairs, out the door, and headed for Bayview Road. The Bay Point Gazette was located in a storefront, two doors away from the Bay Point police headquarters. Peggy went in. A bell on top of the door tinkled.

Peggy walked into a small front area containing only a table and two chairs. Behind an open door in the back, Peggy could see a big room. There were several desks with typewriters and a large machine she supposed was a printing press. Three or four people bustled about, pounding the typewriters or working the press. One of them looked up at the sound of the bell and came out.

"Can I help you?" The woman seemed rather old to be working in a newspaper office. She had a pleasant, round face and gray-blonde hair pulled back into a bun. Probably a secretary or something, Peggy thought.

"I'm looking for A. Flaherty," Peggy told her. The woman nodded. "That's me. Aileen Flaherty."

Peggy's eyes widened. Nothing was ever the way one expected it to be! She had pictured "A. Flaherty" as a sharp aggressive young man with short black hair and horn rimmed glasses. She had even given him a first name in her mind—*Artie*. Certainly not *Aileen!* "Are you the reporter who wrote the article about the fire on Blount Street yesterday?" she asked.

Aileen Flaherty nodded. "Why do you ask?"

"That was my neighbor's house," Peggy told her.

"That's too bad," the woman said. "And your name is?"

"Peggy Gorman. And there's a lot left out in your article."

Aileen Flaherty's smile disappeared. "Such as?"

"Such as how bad the fire was and how it was set to get rid of the black family living there."

"Are you claiming it was arson?"

"Yes," Peggy said. "And I know who did it!"

"I think we'd better sit down," said Aileen Flaherty, indicating the chairs. She picked up a pencil and a large, yellow lined pad. "Is it okay if I take notes?"

"Sure!"

"Then tell me all about it," the reporter said, and Peggy did exactly that. She described the party at Sandra's house and the threats that had been made there. She told about seeing Harris and the other boys in the car when they hurled the rock through the Purvis' window.

"Harris Wilkerson? The Chief's son?"

Peggy nodded. "And I saw the same kids moving through the bushes just before the fire."

The reporter paused in her scribbling. "Why didn't you give this information to the police?"

"I did!" Peggy said. "I told Chief Wilkerson himself."

Aileen Flaherty's eyebrows shot up in surprise. "That's odd!" she remarked. "The police report where I got the information for the article said nothing about possible arson."

"It's not only possible!" Peggy insisted. "It's certain. Even one of the firemen said so."

The woman shook her head. "And are you saying also that the fire was more extensive than we reported in the story?"

"You bet!" Peggy exclaimed. "Lots of people were there. Ask any of them. Go see the house for yourself!"

Aileen Flaherty put down her pencil. "I intend to do just that." Her mild blue eyes were suddenly alight with excitement. She stood up and so did Peggy. "Thank you Peggy Gorman," the reporter said. "The police won't be able to ignore the front page story I'm going to do on this." She shook Peggy's hand warmly. "You've done the right thing, Peggy."

As Peggy left, she could hear Aileen Flaherty calling to someone in the back. "Get me a photographer right away. We've got a big story to cover!"

Outside, Peggy stared at the nearby police department. "I've got you now, Harris Wilkerson!" she whispered. Then she set out for home, feeling about ten feet tall. Feeling, in fact, just like Doris Day!

Peggy told her parents what she had done. She was afraid they might be upset with her. Instead, her dad whistled with appreciation. "I'm proud of you Pumpkin," he said.

Her mother hugged her. "Me, too!"

Later that day, Julia called from the motel. She wanted to describe in detail the new outfits she had bought, but Peggy insisted that her own news was more important.

"What could be more important than clothes?" asked Julia.

Peggy described her visit to the newspaper office. Julia was so impressed she even postponed the conversation about her shopping trip, and they spent the rest of their time on the phone talking about Peggy's exploits and what could happen next.

"Those boys are going to get what they deserve!" Peggy exclaimed.

"And anyone else who was involved," added Julia. "It wouldn't surprise me if Sandra had something to do with it, too."

Peggy was silent for a moment. She didn't really think that Sandra would do something as terrible as this. She figured it was Harris and his buddies. Either way, however, Peggy was sure that no one in that crowd would ever talk to her again. Surprisingly, that thought didn't bother Peggy too much. *I've come a long way,* she thought. *I'm not scared any more.*

Julia came over the next afternoon. They sat on the porch and waited until the paperboy came by and the newspaper landed with a *thwack* on the porch floor.

And there it was, right on the front page as promised. *DEVASTATING FIRE ON BLOUNT STREET*, the headline screamed. *LOCAL TEENS QUESTIONED IN ARSON INVESTIGATION.*

CHAPTER SEVENTEEN

Two days later, the girls were in Peggy's room chattering excitedly and trying to decide what to wear on the first day of school. The record player was turned up high and a singer's high-pitched voice filled the air.

"Who is that?" asked Julia.

"That's Bob Dylan. He's new. This is his first record. Isn't it great?

They listened to the words.
How many roads must a man walk down?
Before you call him a man?
The answer my friend is blowin' in the wind.
The answer is blowin' in the wind.

"Wow!" Julia exclaimed. "That is really

groovy!"

Julia had brought over a large shopping bag filled with her new clothes. She laid a pleated skirt on the bed, then stopped and looked around. Peggy was pulling a blue denim jumper over her head when she noticed that Julia had become stone quiet and was gazing into the far corner of the room.

"Are you thinking about what happened to us in that closet?" Peggy asked.

Julia nodded. "Those words—*blowin' in the wind*—somehow they made me remember. We were sort of blown by a wind, weren't we?"

Peggy grinned. "You're right! But it must have been really strong to send us so far!"

"More like a hurricane!" Julia agreed. "Did it really happen, Peggy?"

"I often wonder about that." Peggy pulled the fabric of the jumper, trying to adjust the fit. "This feels tight," she commented. "I don't think I can wear it any more."

"But what do you really think?" Julia insisted. "About what happened in that closet?" Peggy bit her lip. "I believe it happened."

"Me, too," Julia agreed. "But if we told anyone, they'd say it was just a dream."

"How could two people have the same dream at the same time?" Peggy pulled off the jumper and tossed it in the growing pile of stuff to be given away.

Mrs. Gorman's voice came floating up the stairs. "There's someone here to see you, Peggy."

"We'll be right there." Peggy quickly put on shorts and a tee shirt, and the girls went downstairs.

Pete and Kimberly were standing in the front hall. Kimberly looked cute in pink capri pants with two matching barrettes in her curly golden locks. Pete had on a tee shirt with the legend *Bay Point Sharks* printed across the front. Peggy recognized it as the name of a local baseball team.

"Hi," Pete and Kimberly said in unison.

Peggy returned the greeting. "Hi. Pete, you've met Julia. Kimberly, this is my friend Julia.

"We were wondering if you heard about Harris," Pete said.

"The newspaper just said that some teenage boys are being questioned," Peggy replied. "They didn't give any names because of their ages."

"The older boys have been charged with arson," Pete told them. "Harris turned them in.

His father made him."

"What's happening to Harris?" Julia asked.

"He's only thirteen," Kimberly said. "So he's not going to jail, but his parents have to pay a large sum of money to the Purvises."

"Chief Wilkerson is furious." Pete remarked.

Peggy nodded. "I'll bet he is! He tried hard enough to cover it up!"

"Maybe he'll be fired," Julia suggested hopefully.

Pete shook his head. "I don't think so. He's part of the crowd that runs the town. But I heard he's really embarrassed, and angry at Harris. That kid will probably be grounded for the rest of his life."

"There's more!" exclaimed Kimberly. "The judge is making Harris write a 25 page report about civil rights and the history of slavery in America." She paused for a moment, then spoke to Julia in a flurry of words. "We're sorry about what happened and we wanted you to know that we...that you..."

Pete completed the thought. "That you are welcome here."

A beautiful smile lit up Julia's face. "Thanks."

"What about Sandra and her other friends?" Peggy asked.

"We're just speaking for ourselves," said Pete. "Sandra and her real close buddies . . .well, they just won't accept that this is the 1960's. Things are different now." He shook his head sadly. "I guess there are some people in town who still don't get it."

"My parents told me I'm not allowed to hang out with Sandra and Harris anymore!" Kimberly exclaimed.

"My folks feel the same way," Pete exclaimed. "But I don't need that crowd. My baseball buddies are okay, and there'll be other kids in school."

"We just wanted to tell you," Kimberly added.

Peggy invited them to stay, but they said they had to leave. Pete had a ball game in half an hour, and Kimberly had a piano lesson.

"Well," Peggy said after they had gone. "What do you think of that?"

Julia grinned. "I don't think we are going to have problems in junior high school after all, girl. Do you?"

"No," Peggy agreed. "It looks as though we'll have a few friends at least." She had been ready to fight the whole world on Julia's behalf, even if that meant losing out on fun times with the "in" crowd. But that might not be necessary after all. Things could be working out for her just as they always did for Doris Day. The thought of her favorite actress brought Peggy's mind around to a more immediate topic. "Talking about school," she said to Julia. "Let's make the big decision." She examined the clothes she had laid out on the bed. "What do you think?"

But Julia had wandered off into space and was staring at the closet again. "How come that hasn't been fixed yet?" she asked.

"We had to wait until the insurance guy saw it," Peggy explained. He was here this morning, and my dad said the contractors will begin the job tomorrow."

Julia strolled over to the closet and peered inside. Peggy followed, wrinkling her nose. It still smelled smoky. The blackened walls looked like bombed out buildings she had seen in old movies. Pieces of charcoal-grey plaster had piled on the floor together with a coating of ashes.

"I believe with all my heart that we saved Titus," Julia remarked. "Right here in this room."

"I hope you're right. I try to think of him free and happy." Peggy stared at the mess. "But we'll never know. It's all gone now."

A mewing sound and a furry head rubbing against her ankle made Peggy turn around. "Look!" she exclaimed. "It's Patches. He isn't even afraid of the closet any more."

Far from being fearful, the cat began to investigate the interesting black stuff on the floor. He poked into a mound of ashes with his paw and pushed some of it aside.

"Hey! What's that?" Peggy exclaimed.

"What?" asked Julia.

Peggy pointed to something that was sticking out of the debris. She bent down and pulled it out all the way.

It was a book. Excitedly, the girls began to brush off the crust of cinder and ashes until the name on the cover was clear. Peggy and Julia looked at each other, shocked and bewildered. It was *Uncle Tom's Cabin* by Harriet Beecher Stowe.

Peggy carried their find into her room where

the light was better and leafed through the pages. They were somewhat yellowed, but otherwise the book looked exactly as it had when she and Julia read it to Titus. Had only a couple of weeks passed since that terrifying day in the secret room, or was it really more than a century ago?

"Look!" Julia exclaimed.

A piece of paper had fallen out of the book and fluttered to the floor. Peggy bent down and picked it up gingerly. With trembling hands, she unfolded the paper. It was a note addressed to Mrs. Woodhouse and dated September 6, 1859. The print was large, almost like that of a child who had just learned to write. But the words were correctly spelled and clear to read.

Dear Mrs. Woodhouse,
Several years have passed since last we met, but I have never forgotten you. As you can see, I can now read and write. I learned a trade and have a good job. Most important of all, I am free, thanks to you and the others at your station. I will always be grateful and wait for the day when all my brothers and sisters will know the joy of freedom.
Titus

For a long time, the girls were silent, each

wrapped in her own thoughts and memories. Finally, Julia spoke.

"If we show this to people, no one will believe that we were actually there."

"It doesn't matter," Peggy said. "We know it."

"And what's more," Julia added eagerly. "We know what happened to Titus. Oh, Peggy, isn't it wonderful?"

The girls hugged. They laughed and they cried, knowing that they would be friends forever. Then they returned to the task of choosing clothes for that all-important first day at junior high.

Carol H. Behrman

CPSIA information can be obtained at www.ICGtesting.com
265433BV00001B/6/P